HEAVEN, INDIANA

HEAVEN, INDIANA

· · · · · · · · · · · · · · · · · · · ·

Jan Maher

Dog Hollow Press

Seattle, Washington

DOG HOLLOW PRESS
P. O. Box 22287, Seattle, WA 98122-0287
206-568-1195 PHONE & FAX
1-866-568-1195 TOLL-FREE
www.doghollow.com

Design and production:
Deb Figen, Art & Design Service, Seattle
206-725-2892 / artdesign@jps.net

Cover photo:
Library of Congress Prints and Photographs Division

Publisher's Cataloging-in-Publication
(Provided by Quality Books, Inc.)

Maher, Jan.
      Heaven, Indiana : a novel / by Jan Maher. -- 1st ed.

      p. cm
      ISBN 0-9703993-0-8

      1. Indiana--Fiction.   I. Title.

PS3563.A3575H43 2000   813'.6
                                  QBI00-901482

FIRST EDITION
Printed in Canada
03 02 01 00   4 3 2 1

. . . .

For all the Miller girls

. . . .

ELEPHANTS PACED RESTLESSLY, their immense feet beating slow syncopations. Monkeys gossiped nervously of fearsome and forbidden places. Chameleons flicked their quick tongues and tasted the August air. An unblinking boa curled round the single rock that graced its cage; the tiger mother bared her teeth and readied her claws.

Out on Millstone Road, up in Lester and Helen Breck's barn, daughter Melinda howled in surprise, then roared in rage. Pain had taken her past exhaustion to a point of pure compelling necessity. Angry at the wrenching labor, this betrayal by nature, she took a great gulp of air and finally expelled her squalling daughter. Rough hands guided the infant upwards to her mother's belly, placed her at the breast. The anonymous babe turned her lips, seeking the nipple, and laid claim to her first meal.

Around the corner and down the road, the Wild Animal Caravan of the Hoosier Midways Carnival, mysteriously persuaded that the worst of some invisible storm was now over, finally settled down to sleep at the Heaven, Indiana 4-H and Fair Grounds.

· · ·

There was a distracted air about this new mother. She was the farmer's daughter immortalized in bad jokes about traveling salesmen. Her own bad joke had passed through a little over eight months earlier, leaving samples all over central Indiana. One grew in the belly of Melinda — not a particularly bright girl, but a pleasant and obedient one. She'd been instructed by her father to make up the extra bed for the Fuller Brush man. "I'd like the gentleman to feel at home," he'd said.

The peddler knew an opportunity when he saw one. "You know what would make me feel most at home?" he asked the innocent Melinda. "I've got a pretty little wife there, and she keeps me warm at night. If you really want to make me feel at home, you could come back later, after your folks is asleep, and cuddle up here with me for a bit, so's I'm not so lonesome."

Melinda enjoyed this seduction. It was different, doing it in a bed. The brush man was a far more accomplished lover than Cedrick Burney, her classmate across the border of the back forty. She didn't think to consider what might happen next.

By the time Melinda's surprised roar pushed her infant into the Midwest world, she'd been sequestered for fully four months — kept in the barn by her mother, who told friends and neighbors that Melinda had gone to Iowa to help an ailing great aunt. Seventeen weeks in the barn had changed the farmer's daughter. She'd grown more and more to trust the ways of cows and pigs, less and less to expect anything of mothers.

It was her father who tended the birth.

Helen Breck did come out to take a look at the newborn, and found her worst fears confirmed. So when Lester came to tell her that Melinda had developed a fierce fever in the pre-dawn hours of her second day postpartum, Helen did what had to be done. A woman no longer given to tears, having long ago learned that they got her nothing but more grief, she was determined not to cry. She wrapped the infant in a clean piece of flannel, put it in a picnic basket and put the basket in the Kaiser. "Bring Melinda in the house," she told Lester, "and give her as much hot chamomile tea as she can take. I'll be back in a bit." And she drove off to town.

Lester was afraid to ask his wife where she was intending to go. These past many months he'd felt unable to ask her about anything she was planning, had preferred instead to wait and see. The tortured determination on Helen's face the day she sent Melinda to the barn had chilled him, made him suddenly fearful of something he couldn't name. The keen intelligence and wry wit he loved in her had given way to humorless hypervigilance. Now she carried herself coiled, ready to spring, and it kept him in a state of constant, unfamiliar anxiety.

He'd protested at first. "Don't you think she'd be better off in one of those homes, Mother?"

But Helen would hear none of it. "How will she take care of herself? No stranger is going to look after her as well as we can."

"Couldn't she just stay in the house, then?"

"Now how long do you think it would be till the whole town knew? She has enough trouble with people taking advantage without these young fellows around here getting the idea they can have their way with her."

Lester had to admit that she had a point. Helen had always been fiercely protective of Melinda, and Melinda was pretty dependent on them. This did seem to be a way to manage the situation without getting all of Heaven in an uproar over it.

So instead of arguing further with Helen's decision, he'd done his best to make the girl comfortable in her exile. He set up the rollaway bed for her, built a little table and bench, brought out an extension cord to run off the light in the chicken coop so she could see after the sun went down, hauled up the old platform rocker so he could sit sometimes and keep her company. He brought her books to look at, quilt patches to work on, and a Ball jar full of fireflies with holes poked in the lid — hoping it would amuse her as much as it had years before, when she had tried to read by their light.

They didn't talk much about her situation. She never questioned the appropriateness of her punishment. There had been rumors at school the year before about Gloria Montgomery, a girl over in Montpelier, who graduated from high school and went off to social work school in June. Everyone seemed to know that girls didn't go to college and even if they did, no one went in June. It was pretty clear that Gloria had made a big mistake, was "p-g," would be gone for a few months, and would reappear later, slimmer, without a whit more education. Perhaps, Melinda reasoned, Gloria had been sent to a barn, too.

Melinda and her father sat quietly most of the time, or Lester read a bit from the Bible or from Volume D-E-F of the Wonderbook Encyclopedia, which Melinda had bought some years back at an estate sale.

As close as they got to be, though, it embarrassed Lester to be the one she hollered for when her water broke. He had to keep reminding himself that he'd delivered dozens of calves, and this was surely no different.

. . .

At the midway, there was still a hint of dew on the grass, and everyone was sleeping in. The night had been still and hot; sleep hadn't even been an option till well after midnight. Helen took care that no one saw her stop near the tent of Madame Gajikanes, the Gypsy fortune-teller, nor saw her place the basket at the door. Then she got back into the Kaiser and drove on.

She made a stop at Clara's Kitchen, parking up the street so her footpath to Clara's would take her by early-riser Ida Mueller's yard. There, Helen stopped to compliment Ida on her beautiful flowerbeds, and stayed to chat a full fifteen minutes about the winning lima beans at the Centennial Fair. "Fordhooks," Ida said in summary, "are always the best bet."

"That's a fact," Helen agreed. "You can always count on Fordhooks."

At Clara's, she discussed the new elementary school principal with June Wade, who took her order for black coffee and white toast. June had heard he was a young fellow, not much more than thirty. "He'll have his hands full with all those Bickle children running around the hallway," Helen opined.

After breakfast, she strolled up the street to Herman's Market and picked up a loaf of Korn Krust bread. On the way back to the car, she waved through the window of Charlene's Beauty Shop to Minnie, helmeted in the dryer, first customer of the day.

At home again, she checked on Melinda, who was inside now, tossing in her sleep. She sponged the girl's forehead, and cleared away the teacup. Then she went out to the barn, to make sure there were no obvious signs of its having been used as an inn. Lester had put the bed away, moved the rocker back to the porch and brought the books and sewing projects inside. Helen dismantled the extension-cord lighting system and liberated what were left of the lightning bugs. Next, she went to the summer kitchen, where a peck of Kentucky Wonders Lester had picked that morning waited. He had already fired up the old woodstove and started water heating in the canner. She slid the pot aside, lifted the burner, and looked once over her shoulder to make sure he wasn't around to watch. Then she pulled an old photograph from her apron pocket and tossed it onto the bed of burning coals. She watched till flames crawled completely across the image before replacing the burner. Only then did she allow two or three tears to surface before drying her eyes on her apron hem and turning her attention to stringing the beans.

The next day at church she bubbled with news. "Melinda called from the bus station in Marion late last night, back from Sioux City. When we picked her up, she was so tuckered out from traveling that she went right to sleep in the car, hardly even woke up to go to bed, and was still sleeping when we got up for church this morning. Well, we decided to let her just rest up a bit." She dropped her voice and confided, as if telling secrets of state. "You know, it's a two-day trip on the Greyhound. The poor thing is just exhausted."

"Your Aunt Doris is feeling better, then?"

"Oh, yes," Helen said. "Melinda said she's fit as a fiddle now.

"It's a blessing to have family to help you out when you need it."

"Yes, it sure is."

. . .

There's a particular kind of haze that hangs over an Indiana town on a hot August day. It isn't really bright golden, at least not in Heaven. It's almost white.

The fortune-teller slept in her tent that Friday night. Something she rarely did, but there was more air there than in the trailer, and the August heat was so still and pressing that those with any options to do so bedded down where there was at least hope of a bit of breeze.

John and Maggie Quinn Fletcher fled with their chubby, but not yet giant infant to the riverside, where they sat far enough apart to let any wayward breeze circulate freely between them. The baby, a girl, was colicky. Maggie let her suck a finger dipped in whiskey before handing the pint bottle to her husband. Then she raised her skirt over her immense knees and fanned herself with it. John settled his bulk on the bank of the river and sipped the whiskey. Between them they weighed well over half a ton, and August heat was one of their greatest occupational discomforts, if not outright hazards. The baby was, as yet, in the normal weight range, but it, too, was suffering from the heat.

The less kind among their audiences declared it a miracle that John and Maggie were ever able to get near enough to each other to accomplish pregnancy in the first place. But somehow they had, though Maggie had been unaware of her condition until the night of the Memorial Day parade. She had eaten heavily in spite of the heat, her value to the carnival dependent on her ability to top the scales at more than five hundred pounds. An illness earlier that spring had caused her weight to dip precipitously to four hundred eighty-one, and she needed to gain back the lost twenty pounds. Her part of the sideshow involved stepping onto elephant scales for a weigh-in. The scales had initially been altered to keep her above five hundred, but a rare inspection from Weights and Measures that day had required Mr. Coleson, the carnival manager, to correct the "error."

The night of the parade, Maggie thought she had heartburn. When she began to have cramps, John sent for Granny, as everyone called Madame Gajikanes. Granny was known, in addition to her fortune-telling, for having a few tricks up her sleeve: old Gypsy cures, it was said. The carny people were generally willing to put much more trust in their own Granny than in any of the small-town doctors who practiced along the carnival routes.

Maggie's water broke just as Granny arrived, and it hadn't taken her psychic powers to note that Maggie's problem would be fully apparent in a moment and far more chronic than heartburn.

So when Granny awoke from the mugginess and stepped outside her tent that August morning to catch a breath of air, she thought at first that John and Maggie had left their daughter Lenore at the door. It took only a moment to realize, however, that the infant at her feet was entirely new, no more than a day or two old.

Granny didn't hesitate. She brought the basketed baby in. "And who are you?" she crooned to it, as she peeled back the bits of blanket and clothing to see if it was boy or girl who had come visiting. "A little girl? That nobody wants? And nothing to your name. *Nada en todos. Rien de tout.* But that's all right. That's the best way to be. Nothing to hold you down, nothing to keep you back. Let me see your hand, little one." Gently, she pried the tiny fist open. "A strong heart line," she assured the infant. "That's good. You'll need it in this world. And you've got a good long life coming, too." She touched the life line and the baby closed her fist again, holding tightly to Granny's finger. But what struck Granny most about this newcomer wasn't her life line. It was her eyes. They seemed to take in everything.

Madame Gajikanes laid her plans. Old Man Coleson wouldn't want to deal with another infant. He was already in an uproar about John and Maggie, although he grudgingly acknowledged that the child was indeed adding to the value of the sideshow. Not that children were forbidden or even discouraged. They were doted upon by most of the regulars. It's just that Coleson hated surprises and he abhorred scandals.

And Granny knew for a fact that an abandoned baby was somebody's scandal; especially one abandoned at a Gypsy's tent. No matter that Madame Gajikanes wasn't a real Gypsy. The myths were as pervasive as they were fallacious, and Old Man Coleson was obsessive about avoiding trouble. His was a Sunday-school carnival of the first degree. He wouldn't want any headlines about baby-stealing to sully his reputation.

She had, of course, no bottles with which to feed a baby. Maggie did, but Granny couldn't trust her to keep a confidence. Some who knew Maggie best said her mouth was the very biggest thing about her. There was Lillian, on the other hand, whose prize Bengal had just given birth. Granny went to Lillian and told her a child had arrived from heaven.

She left with two bottles and a three-day supply of baby tiger formula. She mixed the formula with one of her own that kept the infant safely quiet in the back room of her tent. Her customers on Saturday and Sunday never guessed that while their secrets were being discovered in the wrinkles of their palms, Granny kept one of her own just a few feet away. And when the photographer from the Heaven Historical Society took a human-interest photo of the town's new babies at the gate to the fairgrounds, with the Centennial Fair and Hoosier Midways forming the backdrop, only two infants were featured: Eleanor Alice, born the tenth of June to Robert and Katherine Denson, and Sue Ellen Sue, born the fifth of January to Frederick and Elizabeth Tipton. The unnamed baby found the twenty-first of August by Nancy White (known to her clients as Madame Gajikanes) went entirely unremarked.

. . .

The sun came up Monday morning on a day that promised little relief from the heat. At the Breck farm, Melinda was too feverish to articulate her consternation. She was fairly sure she'd had a baby, but she couldn't seem to find it. Fitful sleep, strange dreams, flames, images of her skin like parchment paper catching fire at the edge then wafting up in ghostly white ash. "Mother," Lester called out from Melinda's bedside, where he had relieved Helen of the watch at four o'clock, when it was time to feed the chickens and milk the cows. "I think she's taking a turn for the worse."

Helen Breck finally admitted she was out of her league. She called Doctor Brubecker then, and reached his nurse, who told her the doctor was on vacation for another four days. Relieved, she called his backup, who arrived from Hartford City just in time to watch Melinda draw her last breath. Helen professed astonishment when the doctor declared that Melinda appeared to have given birth very recently, and that under the circumstances he'd probably have to order an autopsy. She broke down and sobbed, beat her fists upon her stolid husband's chest and wondered aloud and copiously how Melinda could have done this to them; wondered, moreover, what could have happened to the baby. Even insisted that the Chicago Greyhound station be searched for what would be their first and only grandchild, their only hope of an heir.

. . .

Monday was strike day for the carnival. While the rest of the folks finished folding their tents and packing up their props, Granny announced that she was off for a minute or two to coax her old '38 Chevy to the gas station, fill the tank. And it was as easy as that to slip out of Heaven, go off to find another carnival where no one would question the sudden appearance of a new granddaughter. Later, Lillian, thinking quickly, told a furious Coleson that Granny had gotten an urgent letter from her estranged daughter Peggy on Saturday, and after a long-distance call on Sunday night, had felt compelled to make the trip to Ohio, where her help was needed.

On her way out of town, Granny passed by Sheriff Johnson, headed out to the Breck farm to see what all the fuss up there was about.

. . . .

SHE WASN'T WHAT YOU'D CALL a well-behaved child. For one thing, she changed form constantly. Sometimes she was an infant, sometimes a toddler, sometimes big enough for kindergarten or even first grade. Sometimes she chattered, sometimes she was sullen and mute. Sometimes she looked like Lester's side of the family, blond and blue-eyed; sometimes she favored her hazel-eyed mother; sometimes her eyes darkened more like Helen's and her hair showed hints of being naturally curly. And she drove Helen crazy the way she'd just sit in the corner of the kitchen and stare at her, or worse yet, chant a barely coherent scrap of childhood rhyme. Eeny, meeny, miney, moe, she droned over and over, till Helen thought she would scream.

"Hush, now," Helen would admonish, but the child refused to hush, except when any of Helen's egg customers dropped in. At those times, she disappeared altogether.

And then Lester, who had at least tried to be helpful at the beginning of this nightmare, up and died in an accident exactly six years after Melinda's return from Sioux City. Lucky for Helen that fellow Harley came along looking for work just about the same time, so at least the farm was still operating at full efficiency.

She met him at the cemetery where she'd gone to visit Melinda's grave. She bent down to put some flowers by the headstone and when she straightened up again, it was Lester's name she saw at her feet. She turned to the kind-looking stranger nearby and announced, shocked by the suddenness

11

of fate into an uncharacteristically quavering voice, "My husband's dead."

"Not hardly," Lester assured her.

"Harley," Helen repeated, trying to remember if she'd ever met this fellow before.

"Hardly dead," Lester said. "Why, I'm standing right here, Mother."

Helen stared a moment, then looked around wildly. Lester could tell something was very wrong.

"Are you all right?"

"I'm a little nervous, to tell you the truth."

"Can I do something to help?"

She looked at the grave. It looked back at her.

"I wonder if you wouldn't mind giving me a ride home," she said, surprising herself with the boldness of it. It wasn't like her to ask anyone for favors, let alone perfect strangers. "I don't know if I ought to drive right now." She looked up at the sky, as if she expected lightning to strike. And if she wondered why this man had no car of his own, she kept it to herself.

As Lester held the car door open for her, she managed to remember her manners and thanked him. "Harley Dade? You must not be from around here. I never heard of any Dades in Hutter County."

Lester wasn't sure what to say. They rode in silence to the main road.

"It's up left about two mile," Helen directed him.

He ventured to ask how her husband had died, and listened while Helen filled him in on the details of his own presumed death. They coincided precisely with the particulars of Omar Breck's death, Lester's father. Pops had died back in '49 in a grim combine accident.

When they turned up the driveway, Helen sighed. "I don't know what I'm going to do now. That hay needs baling."

Lester glanced across at her. He decided to play along for the time being. "I reckon I could get that done for you."

"You know how to run a baler?"

"Yes, ma'am."

"I don't have a lot to pay."

"Well, I don't really need a lot. Just a place to put my head at night and meals is all. Maybe a little bit of cash for my Mail Pouch and a cuppa coffee in town now and then." It was the same compensation he'd always worked for.

She hired him on.

Lester thought about it while he chewed a comfrey leaf and rode the John Deere through the rows. Seemed to him like this was how Helen had decided to deal with guilt. Like someplace deep inside her she believed she was being punished for abandoning the little baby girl, and she'd translated that into some kind of figuring that she didn't deserve happiness, or a husband, or much of anything. Lester hoped that if he just humored her, she'd come back to herself. Maybe then she'd laugh, thinking about how she mistook his reassurance for the name Harley Dade. It surely had been a long time since he'd heard her laugh.

In the meantime, he accepted the situation as his own punishment. He didn't want to let himself expect too much, or want too much. He too had sinned, and it was fitting, even necessary, that he pay for it.

Helen, he knew, had been haunted about her choices almost from the beginning. Within days of her impulsive decision to drop the child at the tent stoop of the Gypsy fortune-teller, she'd started looking for Hoosier Midways. But in the whole long six years, that particular carnival had not returned to Heaven, nor had it appeared in any other nearby community.

The first week after Melinda died, the doctor, as obligated by law, had filed a death certificate at the Hutter county seat. The Brecks, mindful of this requirement, had done their own reporting, calling the local sheriff to ask aid in contacting agencies and officials in Chicago and Sioux City. Lester Breck suffered for these deceits, but he'd long ago relinquished all decisions related to child-rearing and business to his wife. Now was certainly no time to question her wisdom. Besides, he knew enough to figure that since he had tended Melinda's labor, and hadn't insisted on medical attention for her when she started to fail, he was probably guilty of something under the law, not just in his own conscience. And he wasn't prepared to live as an outright criminal either in or out of jail. He valued his acreage and his camaraderie at the Grange. He valued hot breakfasts at Clara's Kitchen before sunup. He valued Indiana sunsets and a plug of Mail Pouch while riding the tractor.

So cooperating authorities searched the Chicago bus and Sioux City bus stations, and interviewed Helen's Aunt Doris. When Doris said no, she'd never even seen Melinda, Helen fainted so convincingly that the sheriff figured the girl had deliberately deceived her mother to hide her shame. For Helen had shown him letters the girl had written. And they were in her handwriting (the conscientious sheriff had checked, even though he regarded the Brecks as salt-of-the-earth citizens). Once a week, Helen had dictated to her barnbound daughter what to write about life in Sioux City, and had shared those letters with enough people that it was generally accepted as true that they were written and mailed from there. Eunice Switzer even remembered a Sioux City postmark, although she'd actually never seen an envelope.

When the official investigation died down, Helen set about her own discreet mission to locate the infant. "Our only hope," she told folks, "is to take it to God." She went to church each week and asked Him, but said that in the meantime, while she waited for His answer, she wanted to consult that fortune-teller as well. "I heard that the one with the carnival this year really has a gift. Didn't she tell Eunice Switzer exactly where to find her lost ring?" But no one seemed to know for sure where the carnival had gone.

Ida said she thought there was usually a carnival in Muncie by Labor Day, but Helen made the drive in vain. No one she talked to in Muncie could remember a carnival having been there for at least three or four years. Of course, Helen didn't want to seem to be too fixated on that particular fortune-teller, so throughout that winter she consulted palm readers in Fort Wayne and Richmond, an astrologer in Indianapolis, and a numerologist in Marion. The next summer, and for five summers thereafter, Lester dutifully drove her to visit every fortune-teller at every county fair or carnival within a hundred miles of Heaven. None of them was named Gajikanes. Helen asked each of them, nonetheless, about the lost child. All of them spoke in soothing generalities. Helen regarded them all, to a woman, as fakes.

On the twenty-first of August, they visited the Huntington Fairgrounds and spoke with a crystal-ball-gazer whose sole insight was, "Sometimes, near is far and far is near." Something in Helen snapped. She sat silent all the way from Huntington through Marion. When they passed the farm stand in Gas City she told Lester to back up and get some flowers, she wanted to visit Melinda's grave. Lester might have worried right then, if he had been a worrying man. She hadn't been to the cemetery since the funeral.

Of course, after Helen announced Lester's death to Minnie, there was some talk. Lester took Minnie aside and explained, as much as he was willing to, what had happened. "I'd appreciate it," he said, "if you kept it to yourself for now. Just in case she snaps out of it, you know, I don't want her to feel embarrassed."

"Oh, you can count on me," Minnie said, and when she confided in Ida she asked for the same assurances.

Ida didn't tell a single person, other than just to mention it to Eunice. "Poor soul," she said, and Eunice nodded. Maybe it was her husband Earnest who overheard and didn't have the sense to keep it quiet. However it happened, it wasn't long till most of the town knew. But when they saw Helen in church, she looked so normal. She sang the way she always sang, she put two dollars in the collection tray the way she always did. And back on the farm, she continued to function in all the various ways she had over the years. The eggs she traded were just as fresh, the bills paid just as promptly. So no one felt it necessary to interfere with this insistence on treating Lester as her hired hand. As long as her husband was willing to put up with her, they figured, it wasn't for them to get involved.

Except, of course, they did keep an eye on the situation, just in case. After all, what are neighbors for, if not to keep an eye out? "You never know," Minnie would say to Ida.

"That's right," Ida would reply. "You never do."

Even Eunice, who usually did all her shopping at Herman's, started buying eggs from Helen, so she could check on her at least once a week. She tried to find ways to linger and look around on her egg days, but Helen had a way of discouraging that.

She tolerated the hovering of her friends, but Helen was happiest when she was alone. She even managed to discourage the little ghost of a girl, who, as the months went by, grew dimmer, but never older now.

Sometimes Helen stood at the kitchen window and watched Harley on the tractor. She liked to watch him because he walked like Lester, talked like Lester, used the same gestures, even sounded the same when he sneezed during hay-fever season. She kept these observations to herself, however, not wishing Harley to get any improper ideas. He was, she was relieved to note, a gentleman. Once in a while, he'd overstep his boundaries and ask about something he had no business asking about, or tell her she was looking particularly attractive that day, but he always backed right off when she let him know he'd crossed that line.

• • •

Hanging on the wall of the one restaurant in Heaven is an embroidered sampler that reads:

Monday's soup is full of peas
Tuesday's soup contains some cheese
Wednesday's soup has lots of tomatoes
Thursday's soup has beets and potatoes

Friday's soup is minestrone
Saturday's soup has macaroni
Sunday's soup's the very best
'Cause Sunday is our day of rest
See you in church!

At the bottom, the needle artist had cross-stitched a little white church with a steeple and a wisp of smoke coming from the chimney. Beneath the sampler, in careful block lettering on a piece of stiff shirt cardboard, hung another, somewhat more recent message:

Now Open on Sundays —
Serving Chicken Noodle Soup with All Dinners.

Clara's Kitchen hadn't been run by Clara for a couple of years, but when Stella took over she thought it wouldn't really be respectful to change the name. After all, Clara had put her life into the little cafe, doing all the cooking and serving at first, and setting her hours to accommodate everyone possible. If she had given it up due to death, maybe Stella would have called it Stella's Place, but Clara was just retired. So to honor her, Stella kept the name and menu as they'd always been.

Most of Stella's customers were regulars. She had some ideas for building up the business — bringing in more customers from nearby towns and getting more of Heaven's families to eat dinner out once in a while. But she didn't mind that breakfast was usually slow. She enjoyed having the time to sit sometimes and chat with the fellows who came in faithfully for their morning coffee and sweet rolls. The home-baked sweet rolls were one of the two specialties Stella had added to the menu, the other being rhubarb coffee cake when rhubarb was in season. Stella had a huge patch of rhubarb.

This morning, Lester was holding forth for her benefit and that of Maurice Wilson and Bobby Bennett. Away from home, Lester was a gregarious, garrulous man, and Clara's Kitchen was for him a lifeline. Helen never liked people "poking around" her house, as she put it. If she had something to say, she'd come to you. And she didn't have a whole lot to say these days. What she did have, she saved for her once-a-month visit to Charlene, her hairdresser. Then too, she certainly didn't expect a hired hand would have the audacity to invite people to her house. No, he could just go on down to Clara's if he wanted to set around shooting the breeze with a bunch of fools.

Lester was nostalgic today, and feeling philosophical. The conversation had somehow turned to fireflies, and everyone had a story to tell about how, as kids, they had collected them. Maurice remembered the mysterious glow it made when you stepped on one and smeared it across a patch of concrete.

When it came to Lester's turn, he settled back in the booth and shook his head slowly at the preciousness of his memory.

"There's a way of watching lightning bugs takes you right out of this world. You set on your porch, or out in a lawn chair, and begin to pick 'em up just about a half hour after sunset. By ten or so they're all over the place. One here, then it goes out and the next thing you know it's over there. Or maybe it's a different one this time. It takes your mind right out watchin' 'em. They're like stars. Like they say about stars, being born and dying all the time all through the ages, only lightning bugs are right in your own yard.

"When Melinda was just a little thing I remember taking her to the county library once. There was this fellow — well, I suppose he must've been a librarian — asked the kids what were they curious about. Well sir, I didn't wait for the kids to answer. I just piped right up and said lightning bugs. What about 'em, he says. Well, how they do that, I says. How they light up. So he looked it up right on the spot. Now I don't remember what the explanation was. But I remember he said folks down in the jungle in South America got lightning bugs so big they strap 'em on their shoes so they can see at night." He paused, and got a distant look in his eye. "When Melinda heard that story about lightning bugs as big as flashlights, her eyes got just about that big too and she wanted some on her own shoes. Wondered why we couldn't just hop on down to South America and get a few."

Stella wasn't sure it was a good idea for Lester to get started on Melinda stories. She'd seen him before like this. He'd start with what seemed like a happy memory of his daughter, and before you knew it, he'd get a dark look in his eyes and settle into silence. And silence was not Lester's natural, healthy state. She asked, "Warm your coffee, boys?" and filled all the cups, then announced that she had to get the soup started for lunch.

That galvanized everyone. They stood, downed their last cup in a few long swigs, and headed out the door — Lester to harrow his winter wheat field, Maurice to ready Heaven's Bread for the day's business, and Bobby to open his service station. ("If you don't like the service in Heaven," the motto on his custom-printed wall calendars said, "you can go to Hell." Some folks thought it was sacrilegious to have a motto like that, but Bobby kept his own copy of the calendar in his jumbled and greasy shop area where customers weren't allowed and women preferred not to set foot anyway. He mailed the others out in plain brown wrappers to his best customers, and they kept them tucked away in garages and workrooms.)

"Bye, fellows," Stella called after them as they banged through the screen door. Stella exhaled, and headed to the kitchen to chop up the onions. Clara's Kitchen was momentarily empty.

Later that night, Lester dared to reminisce again. "Remember that time when Melinda was little and I took her to hear about the lightning bugs?" he asked Helen.

"What are you talking about," she snapped. "You never took her anywhere when she was little. Why, I never even met you till she was twenty-two and six years dead."

Lester nodded. "Well, I reckon I ought to get on to bed."

"Don't forget to turn the light out." Helen gathered her mending and headed upstairs.

"No, ma'am."

. . . .

SHE SITS IN A SWING suspended by long uneven chains and dusts her toe in circles in the hollow place in the dirt. Then twists to her right until the chains are tightly coiled and her toe barely reaches the ground to hold herself in place. Finally, she lets go her toehold, flings her head back — lean arms outstretched, lanky legs extended, balanced confidently on the ribbed metal seat — and enjoys the dizzying ride back to normalcy. When the swing reaches equilibrium again she repeats the process, this time twisting to the left. Nadja always likes to keep things balanced.

A stocky, freckled girl with a sunburnt nose approaches cautiously, sidles onto the swing next to Nadja, and begins unwrapping a Milky Way. She, too, dangles toes in the dirt below, and twists side to side. Seeing Nadja notice her treat, she offers, "Do you want half?" Nadja takes a moment to answer, unnerved by the sudden generosity of this stranger.

"Yes," she responds at last. The girl breaks off the unwrapped end of the candy bar and walks her swing toward Nadja's. Nadja accepts the gift wordlessly. Her frank stare flusters the girl, who lowers her eyes and occupies herself with chewing the caramel and chocolate. Nadja eats her half more slowly, thoughtfully. The other girl starts to swing now, pumping hard to gain altitude. As the swing describes its arc to the rear, she sweeps her gaze over the park grounds. To the right are tents, trailers, the evidence of a small carnival passing through. To the left is the merry-go-round, with a single occupant sitting on it; just beyond it, the jungle gym; straight ahead, those treacherous metal bars, hung by chains to a steel maypole of sorts; and past that, the two sliding boards — one for the little kids, one for the big kids.

Swinging forward causes a hard lump in her stomach, a feeling that she may simply fly off her seat and sail over the park, crashing onto the bare hard clay beyond. She considers slowing down, but does not wish to appear a coward to her intriguing companion.

Nadja begins to swing now, too, and soon matches the other girl's pace.

"Are you with it?" she calls out across the space between them.

"What?" the other queries stupidly.

"Are you with the carnival?" Nadja elaborates, already knowing the answer.

Now registering the question, the girl replies, "No."

"I am," says Nadja, and they fall silent for a moment, rhythmic sisters, riding the muggy August air.

After a time, the girl speaks. "I wish I was."

Nadja looks surprised. "Why?"

"I don't know. What's it like?"

"I don't know. It's all right."

"Are you an acrobat?"

"I help my grandmother. We don't have acrobats."

The girl is silent again. If it isn't acrobatics, she hopes it might be lion taming, but this is unlikely to be a grandmother's special trade. "Does she train animals?" she finally asks.

"She reads palms," Nadja answers.

The swings and their occupants continue the back-and-forth arc. Not simply swinging side by side but gathering some kind of energy between them, some palpable thickening, some welling up until Nadja's own fortune-telling gift lands on her full force for the first ti It knocks her off course. Her swing careens dangerously close to the girl next to her, whom she has suddenly seen on a day thirty-two years ahead. "Chicago," says Nadja.

"Huh?"

"You'll live in Chicago. You won't come home for a long time. I saw it in your candy wrapper."

The girl looks straight ahead, swings out once, back once, before she replies.

"My name is Ellie."

Nadja repeats the sound, "Ellie."

"I was named after Eleanor of Aquitaine."

"Who's that?"

"A queen my mom read about in a book. What's your name?"

"Nadja."

"Are you named after anyone?"

"I don't know."

"Can I go with you?" Ellie asks. "Does your grandma need any extra help?"

"I'll ask," Nadja promises. Then, as if hearing the noon air-raid siren blowing all the way up in Fort Wayne, she suddenly puts her heels down in the dirt and scrapes her swing to a halt. "I have to go to lunch."

"Ask her," Ellie says.

Over on the merry-go-round, Heaven's third nine-year-old sits on her leg, writing in her diary.

Dear Diary,

Today my cousin Leanna gave me her Toni dolls. They have brown hair and blue eyes. I'm going to give them both permanets. Or maybe just one good one, like on TV and the other I could esperiment with stuff on.

I'm going to name them Christy and Misty. I think. Or maybe Marilyn and Carolyn. Or Terrie and Sherrie. I like names that rime, espeshully for twins. The first permanet will be for Christy or Carolyn or Sherrie. Depending on what I name her.

I'm to the park and I just saw Ellie with a jipsy.
Your frend,
Sue Ellen Sue

Sue Ellen Sue closes the book and hugs it to her chest as Ellie crosses the playground to sit next to her.

"I saw you with that Gypsy," she says.

"So?" Ellie challenges.

"So does your gramma know?"

"Know what?"

"Know you're talking to Gypsies?"

"I don't know."

"I'm gonna tell her."

"So what?"

"You shouldn't talk to Gypsies. You can get cooties."

"Says who?"

"Everybody knows that."

"So what?"

"So you probably got cooties."

"Shut up."

"I don't have to."

The girls sit for a time in silence. Finally, Ellie begins to shove her foot into the dusty furrow beneath the merry-go-round, causing it to move slightly. Sue Ellen Sue adds her effort. When the merry-go-round is turning just enough to settle them down, Sue Ellen Sue speaks again.

"I got Toni twins today. You want to come and see them?"

"Sure," says Ellie.

"Let's go." Sue Ellen Sue abruptly jumps off the merry-go-round and runs toward her house.

"Wait up," Ellie calls as she runs after.

• • •

It wasn't easy for Ellie to get out of the house. She had to wait until she had been officially tucked into bed and kissed good night. Then, when she was sure that her father had settled into his third vodka tonic and her mother into "Maverick," she slipped out of her pajamas, pulled her clothes back on in the dark, and carried her shoes with her as she stepped quickly and carefully across the hall to the top of the stairs. There, she dropped to her belly and slithered down, keeping her head below the baseboard just in case one of her grandparents came through the middle room. When her grandfather called "Will ya look at that, Reba?" and her grandmother came from finishing up the dishes to watch a round or two of the boxing match on the downstairs TV, she stepped behind the curtains that hung in the middle-room doorway and waited to make sure the coast was going to stay clear. Grandma Reba almost never watched boxing, but for some reason she decided to sit with Lawrence to tut and cluck at the screen tonight.

Ellie slipped into the kitchen, from there into the enclosed back porch, and then out the door. Once in the yard she turned right, crossed the yard to the brick and concrete behind the rental units next door. Then to the alley, up Third Street and across Liberty, and whenever anyone passed she sat down on the yard curb and tried to look like she lived there.

She'd never gone to the park after dark before. Never seen the shapes of Third Street by streetlight. The hardware store at the corner was closed and full of shadows. By the railroad tracks, Pete's Gate hummed and smelled of beer. Crickets called from the yards she passed and lightning bugs seemed to invite a constant straying from the path.

She found Nadja outside the fortune-teller's tent. "Did your mom come?" Nadja asked.

Ellie shook a silent no, then voiced, "I'm alone. Can I stay here a while?"

"I'm working." Nadja's dark eyes swept the small line of people waiting to consult her grandmother — so subtly that Ellie almost wasn't sure that's what she was doing. "You want to help?"

"Sure," said Ellie. "What should I do?"

"Get me a sno-kone. Cherry lime mix. You got any money?"

"Fifty cent. It's enough."

"Get you one too."

When she got back, Nadja was gone. She stood stupidly — a sno-kone in each hand — and felt herself begin to panic. Finally, she saw Nadja coming across the fairgrounds. Nadja signaled Ellie to wait, then circled behind the tent. Ellie watched, and decided to start on her melting sno-kone. She concentrated on eating only the ice so the cherry flavor at the bottom would be even more intense. She crunched ice and vaguely surveyed the waiting line.

"Are you going to ask about where Amy went?" A tall, big-boned woman with perfectly tweezed eyebrows, precisely applied lipstick, and carefully coiffed blond hair talked to the man standing next to her. He looked hot and anxious, his shirttail untucked in back and his plump hands flexing rhythmically into fists.

"'Course I am." He ran his tongue along his bottom lip and swallowed. "Be well worth it if she could tell me that."

"Doncha think she'd be back by now if she wanted to see you again?"

"Don't care what she wants, Charlene. I want to see her."

"Whatever you say, Norman. I just want to know if my Irish Sweepstakes ticket's going to hit."

"What would you do with that kind of money?"

"I'm sure I could think of something. Maybe a vacation in the Bahamas. I'd like to go there."

"Never heard of 'em. Where they at?"

Then Nadja was at Ellie's elbow. "I thought I saw you..." Ellie began, but Nadja cut her off.

"Got my sno-kone?" Nadja stared at the cup of icy syrup Ellie held.

Ellie handed her the soggy paper cup stained red and green, which was beginning to drip.

"Come on." Nadja had an aura of authority about her that Ellie found irresistible. They walked across the lawn toward the big tent. "What did you hear?" Nadja asked.

"About what?"

"The people in line. What did they say?"

"They talked about what they were gonna ask about."

"What did they say?" Nadja grilled Ellie until she had repeated every word she heard as faithfully as possible, and then, glancing back at the line, abruptly ordered her to stay there. Nadja zipped through the crowd. Ellie finished her sno-kone, licked its sticky residue from her fingers. Nadja reappeared, from the direction least expected.

"Where'd you go?"

"I told you I'm working. But Granny said I could take a break now. Let's go ride the Ferris wheel." Nadja led Ellie down the midway, explaining her job as they went: casual eavesdropping, picking up a clue, a name, a concern, anything, and reporting to her grandmother in the back of the tent.

"So she doesn't really tell fortunes."

"Of course she does." Nadja glowered. "You don't know anything about how it's done." Then, seeing the look of devastation on Ellie's face, she softened her tone and added, "That's just like a kind of boost, to get her started. She has a gift. Everybody says so."

"It's a long line," Ellie noted when they got to the Ferris wheel. She was beginning to wonder if it was a good idea to be standing out where the neighbors might see her. What if the Switzers came by?

"That's okay." Nadja took her hand and led her right up to the front of the line where a one-armed man was taking tickets and helping people into their baskets. Nadja whispered something in his ear, and the next thing Ellie knew, he was ushering them to the final available seat. Ellie was in awe.

"Do you get to ride anytime you want to?"

"Not usually."

And then, with a little lurch that tied Ellie's stomach into a knot, they were off, rising above the fairgrounds. Going up was the easy part. Ellie searched above the housetops for her own, but before she could locate familiar landmarks they were on the way down again, and it took all her attention to keep her fear under control. She pretended to be fascinated by the view, so she could turn away from her new friend and close her eyes. It helped quell the nausea. She was glad when the ride was over. She was doubly glad when Nadja said it was time for her to go back to work. They circled around to the rear of the tents that lined the midway, Nadja leading the way, Ellie stuporously excited.

Again Nadja took her hand, and led her in through the back of the fortune-teller's tent. She put a finger to her lips, signaling Ellie to be quiet, and listened at the curtains until she heard Granny say goodbye to her client of the moment. Then she pulled the curtains aside.

"Granny, this is Ellie," she said, and the old woman turned to peer at the girl and pronounce, "Your parents are going to be looking for you soon. You'd better get home before you get us in trouble."

"Can I stay with you?" Ellie asked, but Granny just laughed.

"I'll write to you if you want," Nadja said. She seemed to know somehow that Ellie wouldn't be allowed to play in the park again while the carnival was still in town.

Granny produced a piece of paper, and Ellie wrote her name and address in her best recently learned cursive. "What's yours," she asked, but Granny and Nadja didn't really know yet what their winter address would be, and till then, they'd be on tour, and pretty hard to find.

"Now get on home," Granny commanded.

Ellie sang a little song to herself while she skipped back over the tracks, past Pete's Gate, by Meyer's Hardware, across Liberty, down Third, through the alley and yard. "I have got a brand new friend, brand new friend, brand new friend. I have got a brand new friend, and her name is Nad-ja."

Her heart almost stopped when, just after she'd gotten to the porch, the kitchen lights flicked on. She flattened herself against the wall and waited while her grandmother got a glass of water, then turned the lights out and went back to bed.

Inside, it was harder to get back upstairs, because it involved passing the bedroom door behind which, she knew, her grandparents were now in bed, at least one of them awake. She slipped off her shoes and tiptoed by, stopped behind the curtains to recover her calm, and then crept on to the staircase. Crouching down, she took the stairs slowly, alert to every sound. In the upstairs living room, her parents were watching Johnny Carson. During a particularly big belly laugh, she scooted past the door, into her bedroom, and slid beneath the blankets. Moments later, the show ended, and she heard her mother's footsteps in the hallway, followed by her father's heavy tread.

Long after the rest of the household was asleep for the night, Ellie lay awake, listening to her heartbeat, straining to hear the sounds of the carnival. And she thought about a saying she'd often heard. Which of them, she wondered, she or her new friend Nadja, lived on the wrong side of the tracks?

Two days later, though she knew it was too soon, she asked Grandma Reba if there had been any mail for her. "Are you expecting something?" her grandmother asked.

"No, I just wondered. I just thought it would be nice to get some mail."

"If you write to your cousins in Elkhart, maybe they'll write back to you," Reba suggested.

Ellie didn't remember her cousins in Elkhart, nor was she interested in getting letters from them. She wanted a letter from Nadja, but none ever came.

. . . .

SUE ELLEN SUE STUDIED THE MAGAZINE DIAGRAM, memorizing the rhythm of the spin: spin up, watch, catch, twirl, five, six, seven, spin up, watch, catch, twirl, five, six, seven. When she felt she had it for sure, she put the magazine aside and picked up the shiny baton, so new it still had cellophane around the rubber ends. The rubber was so clean and white that she hated to risk getting a mark on it, so she left the wrapping in place as she practiced the moves. Spin up, watch, catch, fumble, drop, try again. Spin up, watch, catch, clutch, lose a beat but twirl, six, seven, spin up, watch, grab, get mad, throw, pout, sit, try again. Maybe if she stood exactly like the model in the magazine to begin with, it would help. Left hand placed smartly on her waist, fingers pointing front, thumb pointing back, chin up, back straight, right hand near the middle, but not dead center, of the shiny rod, just a little off to give the right balance control, spin up, watch, catch, twirl, yes! And again, up, watch, catch, twirl, gloat, yes!

Satisfied at last that she had mastered the new move, Sue Ellen Sue sat down to record her accomplishment.

"I got a baton today," she wrote in her best handwriting, aware that someone might someday find this interesting, "and I already learned how to toss it and keep it twirling. Which is good because when I get to Consolidated I want to be a cheerleader. You can't practice too much."

She put the journal aside and picked up the baton again. She loved its feel, the hard rubber tips that gave it ballast, made it balance in her hand as if it meant something.

When it was time to go to bed, she took the baton with her, held it against her body while she thought of routines, and of how to fix her hair so it would stay nice while she jumped and twirled.

She could hardly wait.

. . .

Ellie sat with her head pressed to her bedroom wall and listened to the voices of her parents.

"Oh, god, Katie, what did ya feed me? Ya must've poisoned me!"

"I should've."

"Oh, god, Katie, I think I'm dying."

"You're drinking yourself to death. That's what you're doing. I don't have to do a thing. You do it to yourself."

"Ya must've poisoned me."

"It's the booze and you know it."

"Katie, give me a little something to make it feel better."

"There's nothing to give you. You even drank all my vanilla extract."

"Katie, please, give me something."

"Hush now. You want your dad and mom in on this?"

"Kate, Kate, why are you doing this to me?"

"Hush, Robert. Go to sleep. You'll wake Ellie up."

"You hate me, don't you Kate?"

"Go to sleep, Robert."

"I never thought you'd hate me."

"It's after ten. I have to work in the morning. You have to work in the morning."

"I don't know if I'm gonna make it till morning."

"You want me to call Doctor Brubecker?"

"Just get me something to take the edge off."

"You'll get nothing to drink from me, Robert."

"Just a little bit, Honey. Just to take the edge off."

30

"I'll call Dr. Brubecker and they'll take you over to County. But I won't give you a thimbleful to drink. You can kill yourself if you want to, but you won't catch me helping."

"God, it hurts, Katie...it feels like my gut's on fire."

"You know it's your ulcer. You want some milk? I'll get you some milk."

"Can't you put a little whiskey in it?"

"Drop dead."

"Don't say that, Kate. Don't hate me."

"I don't hate you."

Ellie heard the bedroom door open and her mother's feet padding down the hall to the kitchen. Her father's voice called after.

"They shot his head off, Katie. One second he's there, the next thing I know I turn to look and his head is gone."

"Don't start the war stories, Robert," came Kathleen's voice from the kitchen. "I heard 'em all. They don't change anything. They don't make it all right for you to drink like a godforsaken fool."

Footsteps again, from kitchen to bedroom.

"Here's your milk. Drink up."

"He was my friend, Kate. My best buddy. One second he's there an' the next thing I know the slopes shot his head off. I'm looking at a neck. Just a bloody neck."

"Jesus, Mary, Joseph, Robert, that was fifteen years ago. Just go to sleep now. We gotta be up at five-thirty."

"You might as well do that to me."

"Good night."

"Shoot me like they did him. Shoot my head off. It's quicker than what you're doing."

"Jesus preserve me, go to sleep or else I *am* going to call Dr. Brubecker."

"Kate, remember the birds?"

"What birds?"

"The birds that fell out of the trees — Jesus, you were only about seventeen then, weren't you?"

"Sixteen."

"I was robbing the cradle."

"Too young to know better. And you were old enough to know that. You should've left me alone."

"And there you were standing out in front of your house bawling your eyes out, holding that big cardboard box."

"There was so many of 'em."

"And I come up in my old Packard. Remember that big old boat? And there you are holding that box and bawling."

"There must've been twenty or more."

"An' I says 'Whatsa matter?' an' all you can say is 'They're dying. They're all dying.' Jesus Christ, I thought something had happened to all those brothers and sisters of yours."

"I still get upset thinking about it. All those little birds that never got to fly."

"But no, it was them birds. All them dying birds. Is that what you gave me, Katie? DDT or something? You been spraying my food?"

"I should've."

"Jesus Christ, my gut is killing me."

"That's what you need all right. You need Jesus Christ. You need to get down on your knees and ask Him to forgive you. It's the least you could do."

"God forgive me, I'm a drunk."

"Good night, Robert."

Ellie sat awake, staring into the dark. There's a room on the other side of this wall, she thought, and another on the other side of it and then the bathroom and then the house ends. But somehow she couldn't picture it. All she could picture was room after room after room — stretching on forever. And in each room a set of sparring parents: endless pairs of grim, exhausted mothers, sodden sobbing fathers. It scared her. She blinked and shook her head, then pulled back the curtains next to her bed and looked out the window to reassure herself that there something outside this house of mirrors.

Seeing the movement at Ellie's window, Eunice Switzer, whose bedroom was directly across from Kathleen and Robert's, hastily pulled her own curtains shut. Finally, Ellie slid back under the covers and pulled them up to her chin. She lay that way until the 10:45 train whistled by, six blocks from their home. She placed herself on that train and let its steady rhythm rock her to sleep, carry her off to distant dream places.

SIXTH GRADE WAS NADJA'S HARDEST YEAR. They toured till almost October, and then Granny had a falling out with the manager over how he always wanted Nadja to sit on his lap. He owned the winter house they'd stayed in the year before, and Granny didn't want to have anything more to do with him or his carnival, so she and Nadja packed up and found a place to rent on the outskirts of Fort Wayne.

With the late schedule and the move, Nadja didn't get started in school till almost Halloween. The teacher greeted her by asking if anyone ever teased her about her name being White. "No," Nadja replied, perplexed. "Why?"

The teacher chuckled. "Why, because you aren't white," he said. Nadja was stunned. She'd never given any thought to what color she was, but if she had, she'd have thought she was white. She thought pretty much everybody in Indiana was white. Except for the occasional colored people who came to the carnivals, Nadja had never seen anyone other than white people in the towns in which she and Granny stayed. Tommy Nofsinger, in the seat next to her, was quick to react.

"Eeeeuuuwww," he exclaimed, "I'm not sitting by her." And Mr. Stone let Tommy move to a desk on the other side of the room.

It didn't take long that first recess for Tommy to engage his classmates in trying to guess Nadja's background. "I think she's part nigger," opined one little girl who'd moved up from Kokomo. "Look at her hair. It's curly like a nigger's. I know.

I seen them where I used to live."

"Naw," Tommy countered, "she's got slanty eyes. I bet she's a slope."

"What's a slope?" another asked.

"That's who my dad fought in Korea," Tommy rejoined, enjoying his status as expert.

"Maybe she's Indian," suggested a third.

And Tommy turned to call to Nadja, who stood alone on the steps by the school door, watching the others. "Hey, new girl, are you an Indian?" He held his hand up. "How!" Tommy bellowed, causing the circle around him to burst into giggles.

Nadja watched the children in silence. There were questions slamming into her that had been buried so long she'd forgotten how large they were.

Granny had never actually lied, but she'd used her skills over the years to answer Nadja's questions in a way that allowed Nadja to construct her own mythology about who she was, where she came from. Miraculously, this mythology hadn't been tested before, so there'd been no reason for Nadja to alter it.

In her mind, her mother had been an angel — she looked a lot like the small statue of the Virgin Mary that Granny kept in her tent. As far as she was concerned, she had no father. As far as she knew, fathers weren't necessary, even though they were common. In these innocent days, in this innocent place, Nadja was among the most uninformed of young girls. The voices of her new classmates rode the crisp October air to her ears. "Mr. Stone said she lives with her grandma. Her grandma's a Gypsy," announced one authoritative voice, "so she's a Gypsy too."

"Aren't Gypsies white?" asked one naïf.

"Naw, they're colored," said Tommy. "And they're thieves. Watch your lunch money or the Gypsy'll get it."

When she told Granny what happened, and asked if she was a real Gypsy, all Granny would tell her was that she was a gift from heaven, and that someday, she'd tell her the rest of the story. "For now," Granny said, "just do your best.

Mind your own business, and do your schoolwork. Cruelty is its own punishment, just like kindness is its own reward."

In November, when Nadja scored nearly perfectly on the big math test, Mr. Stone called her up to the front of the room. Holding up her paper, with "98%" written at the top, he announced, "One person in this class only missed one question." For a brief moment Nadja's hopes soared. This, she was thinking, would bring her into the circle of acceptance. Mr. Stone was publicly praising her.

But he went on, "The problem with this is that this was a hard test. A lot of these questions were seventh- and eighth-grade level. The next highest score was only 88%. That's how I know you must have cheated." And Mr. Stone held the paper in front of Nadja and tore it to shreds.

Everything was suddenly silent. Even her classmates were speechless. Even Tommy Nofsinger. Inside Nadja's head and body, everything was hot and cold at the same time. Her ears were blazing, her hands were freezing, her chest felt like heavy, hard, hot lead had been poured in, her eyes felt like they were encased in ice cubes.

She saw Mr. Stone's mouth moving, and struggled to hear what he was saying. "I said — " she could hear him now, just barely — "you may sit down now."

In January another new girl joined the class. She was a big girl, taller than anyone else, who weighed in at over two hundred pounds. Everyone knew this fact because Mr. Stone grilled the unfortunate Lenore about it. When she claimed not to know, he took her down to the nurse's office to determine the answer. He christened her "Tiny" and gave her the seat next to Nadja that Tommy had vacated in October.

Lenore kept to herself, as did Nadja, though whenever an activity in the classroom called for partnering, they always worked together. Partly because no one ever asked to work with either of them, partly because Mr. Stone deemed it appropriate.

One day toward the end of April, Lenore surprised Nadja by inviting her home after school. Lenore's mother was a pleasant, talkative woman who fed the girls chocolate-chip cookies and Cokes. She was big, too, with skin that hung in huge folds and flaps from her oversized frame.

"I'm so glad you came to see Lenore," said Maggie Fletcher when Lenore left to get more Cokes. "She told me you're the only one in the class that doesn't make fun of her. Her dad died, you know, and then I got sick and lost so much weight I couldn't work anymore, and it's been hard on her. I used to be a performer, you know. Her dad and I had a circus act. Lenore says you live with your grandmother?"

Nadja nodded.

"What does she do?"

"She's retired," Nadja said, feeling her face flush with the lie. She dropped her gaze and found herself staring at the cookie crumbs that clung to Maggie's apron. Something about them depressed her. They were leftovers, just like the woman who wore them.

"I'd love to meet her sometime. Maybe the two of you could come to dinner."

"I'll ask her," Nadja said, but she knew she'd never mention a word of it to Granny, and when the touring season started up two weeks later she begged Granny to put their furniture in storage and look for a new winter home for the next year.

"Why?" Granny asked.

"I hate it here," Nadja blurted out, and then she cried so hard that all Granny could do was hold her and stroke her hair and tell her over and over that everything would be all right.

. . . .

SUE ELLEN SUE TIPTON AND ELLIE DENSON weren't exactly a logical pair of friends, but they were friends in the way small towns force friendships. Though Heaven had grown slightly since the year of their births, they had still been the only girls in their group at school. Over the years, John Hutter Elementary had acquired only boys at their grade level, and there never were any girls the year ahead of them or the year behind. One girl had come and gone during their fourth-grade year. Her folks had come up from Louisville and gotten jobs in the chemical plant, but then when the plant had to lay a few people off, naturally they had been the first to go. Sue Ellen Sue missed the girl worse than Ellie did, because the girl had liked hair. Her name was Cornelia, and she and Sue Ellen Sue had spent most of that year fussing with each other's hair. Ellie had pretty much kept to herself — her hair tangled easily, and although she liked having someone else brush it, she hated the pain when a tangle suddenly asserted itself against the pull of a comb. And she didn't really care much for combing someone else's hair, either.

She had played with the boys that year, till her teacher asked her to stay after school one day and advised her that it was not ladylike to wrestle with boys, nor to pretend to be a wild stallion eluding their capture. "I think you should make friends with Cornelia," Mrs. Oglesby had whispered to her, even though there was absolutely no one other than her and

Ellie in the room. "And I'd rather not see any more wrestling with boys," she had said aloud. "Understood?"

Ellie had understood.

When Cornelia and her family headed back to Louisville, Sue Ellen Sue, who never needed to be told that it was unladylike to play with the boys, turned her attentions back to Ellie.

Things changed, of course, in middle school. District consolidation preceded Ellie and Sue Ellen Sue's ascent to the higher grades, so their middle-school years entailed lengthy bus rides to a much larger school where Sue Ellen Sue quickly found her niche in the Booster Club. Middle school was, for her, a daily delight in finding like-minded friends. Her natural curiosity about people and her outgoing personality brought her to the center of the social scene. Her journal filled quickly with descriptions of her friends and teachers, tidbits of news about the year's events, comments on the basketball season, strategies for being chosen a cheerleader, lists of exercises and routines she learned and practiced diligently, triumphs such as perfecting her back flip, tragedies such as twisting her ankle.

It was in middle school that Ellie began to collect maps and consider courses. One led north to Chicago, then east to New York. Another tracked via Denver to Los Angeles. Sometimes she imagined going south to the Mardi Gras, sometimes to St. Louis. By day she plotted, by night she dreamt. Each place in her dreams was built on some scrap of information or misinformation, some little bit she'd heard that defined a place. Thus it was that in New Orleans, everyone danced costumed and masked down the middle of the street, even when going to school or work or church or the grocery store. And in Chicago, due to the poem she'd studied in school, slit-throated pigs ran the streets. New York's Empire State Building had something to do with baseball officials, and it stood next to the Statue of Liberty in Central Park. St. Louis was simply full of people meeting. Sad people meeting. Now, when the 10:45 called to her, she had a sense of destination.

Night after night she found herself disembarking in these cities, and when each day she awoke to her mother's early-morning determination, it always took her a few moments to remember where she was.

Ellie hated to wake up. The cities in her dreams had no stultifying schools in them; no sultry summers so hot and humid that comfort was out of the question; no gaunt yet beer-bellied, beery-breathed father; no distant, preoccupied mother; no friendless horizon; no endless series of walls.

"Why can't you wake me up in Chicago someday," she pouted sleepily one morning as her mother stormed around the room, flinging open curtains and turning on the WOWO farm report.

"Because you live in Heaven," groused her mother, pulling the blankets from Ellie's grasp. "Now get up and get going. Breakfast is on the table and I'm late for work."

NADJA PEEKED THROUGH THE PINHOLE in the tent canvas to see who was first today.

A woman stood ready, florid and floral. Her complexion, a jaundiced yellow at its base, was layered with ruddy sunned shades and topped with crimson rouge. Her hair was that peculiar variegated red that can be accomplished only by repeatedly bleaching and dyeing what had once been jet black. Her dress had in it all the same colors as her hair, and a few more to boot. The overall head-to-toe effect was of a sturdy bolt of Hawaiian shirt fabric. Around her neck she wore a silver chain, from which hung a tiny cross that rested slightly askew on her bosom. She was first in line — in fact, the only one in line, other than Granny.

Now that Nadja was an accomplished fortune-teller in her own right, it was Granny who most often worked reconnaissance. This was a new town, one they'd never been to before, near enough to Chicago to have a big city feeling spilling over into it just a bit. The sign in front of the tent gave Nadja ten minutes till opening. Granny was waiting for the floral woman to initiate the conversation.

There was no breeze, very little sound, and the threat of maximum humidity on this already hot day was gathering, pressing around people. It would soon be difficult to move. The whole town was shimmering in heat, and everything seemed slower, more fluid, as if it were all melting.

The woman finally spoke. "Have you seen her before?"

Granny shrugged noncommittally, relieved when the woman took it for a "no."

"I heard she reads the food best. The dirty plates," the woman went on. "That's a new one to me. I didn't have breakfast, but I never washed the dishes last night, so I brought in my dinner plate. I hope it's enough. 'Course it's not exactly the way it woulda been if I just ate and that was that. I was sitting there, doncha know, watching the six o'clock news and eating snap beans from my neighbor's garden, when all of a sudden my husband says there's something on your plate. Food, I says. No, he says, a cockroach. And he reaches over and swats the sports page at my dinner. And the beans go flying every which way and the butter splats in my lap and the mashed potatoes are on the wall and in my hair and god knows where else, but I don't see any cockroach anywhere. He claims he missed it. Says it got away. I think he hallucinated it. Or musta made it up to see if he could get a rise out of me. So anyway, don't know if that's gonna affect what she sees. She might see his business as well as mine. I s'pose that'd be okay with me, though.

"My mom told me I should come see her." She nodded toward the tent. "Says she heard she's just a little slip of a thing — fourteen or fifteen — but they say she fell on her head one day and just started knowing things she's not even old enough to know. And sees it all in the plates. That's a new one, ain't it? Well, if she can tell me if my old man is fooling around I'll consider it money well spent. I need to know what he's up to. Lord, it's hot."

And then the woman lapsed back into silence. Granny waited a moment, harrumphed, "Looks like I could grow roots waiting for this one to open up. I'm coming back later," and slipped off into the crowd.

Nadja inhaled deeply, said a quick and private prayer, and threw her doors open for that day's business. The floral woman surged through the tent door as if borne by a tidal wave. She wasted no time, but launched directly into her question.

"First off," she said, "I heard you read food the best. Is that right?"

Nadja nodded. "Not any food. It's like tea-leaf reading. I read from the pattern left on your plate after you've eaten. Or I can read your palm."

"Well, here's my pattern." The woman reached into her bag and dropped her dirty Melmac plate in front of Nadja.

"It's last night's dinner. Is that okay? It's not much left."

"That's fine," Nadja answered her. "That's all I need."

"So what do you do? You want me to think of a question? Most of you Gypsies do it that way, don't you? Of course, I've never been to a Gypsy before, but that's what they tell me. Now last year I was at a carnival and the woman didn't want questions. She just did palms. But I don't think she was a real Gypsy, if you know what I mean. She was too light-skinned. Plus my neighbor said she's seen her at Marsh's — buying groceries in the morning during the winter, so that means she lives around here somewhere, she doesn't travel on to wherever they go in the winter. Wherever you go. My neighbor works the swing shift, so when she gets off she does her shopping at midnight on the way home."

"Do you have a question?" Nadja leapt gracefully into the small pause in the woman's monologue.

"I got nothing but questions," the woman responded, and inhaled, ready to present a long list.

"I'd like you to ask the most important one. Ask it silently," Nadja said. "Just close your eyes and think of your question for a moment. Don't think of anything else." After a moment she asked, "Do you have that question in mind now?"

The floral woman nodded, her eyes still shut and her mouth still open.

"You can open your eyes now." Nadja looked intently at the plate in front of her. The floral woman watched.

"This is interesting," Nadja began. "You see this pattern here?"

"That was the mashed potatoes and gravy."

"There was some kind of conflict here, but it wasn't over anything important. Over a...over a bug? Is that right? A fairly large...I'd say a beetle or a cockroach."

The woman kept what she hoped was a steady, noncommittal gaze. She knew that if you responded too much, they might just be telling you things that you were giving away, instead of really using their psychic powers. Nonetheless, she was dumbfounded.

"But it wasn't really about a bug. There was some-one...trying to get your attention."

"Yes..." the woman answered carefully, feeling a little shiver on the backs of her arms in spite of the heat.

"There's a web here," said Nadja, tracing above the pattern with her finger. "A web can mean safety or a web can mean deceit."

The woman looked stricken.

"A web can also mean that someone gets caught. I would say in this case that it is a man. But sometimes being caught is what we want. You see what I mean?"

The woman nodded her head slowly. She looked as if her oversized hairdo was pressing her head down to her chest. As if she might be about to fall forward right onto the plate.

"See this spot?"

"The beet juice."

"It's like a man is trying to get away from the web, but he can't because it's all around him. He has been deceitful in some way — or maybe he's only been suspected of deceit — and now he feels he must leave. But I don't think he wants to leave. He wants the web to close so that he is secure. Does this answer your question in any way?"

"It might."

"There is another shape, in front of him. I think it must be you. I think it means you should talk to him and ask him what he feels bad about."

"What happens then?"

"That depends on you and your husband. It is your husband, I'm sure now. Especially since this is last night's plate. A plate can show you what is, and what has already happened. But it can never say for sure what the future is because people can always change. Otherwise there would be — " she looked straight into the woman's face, " — no free will. And there is always free will. There is no future that you cannot change with your free will, good sense, and love."

"Tell me the truth, miss. Is he going to leave me?" The floral woman gave up any pretense now of skepticism. Her voice quivered in fear.

"See these other spots on the plate? These are other people — family and friends. This part over here looks like the globe. This means there are many people who care for you. For both of you. And there is also a big world to be in. If he wants to be in the world, maybe you can go with him. If you can't go with him, you will still have many people who care about you. Your neighbors perhaps, your mother, your minister. Are there people like this around you?"

"My god, how do you know all this stuff?"

Nadja smiled sadly. "It's just a gift," she said.

"Is there such a thing as too much color?" the woman asked suddenly.

"Too much color?"

"I want to know if there's such a thing as too much color in a person's clothes."

Nadja stared at the plate. "Your essential color is red. That, by the way, is the color of your husband here. That means you have a lot of influence over him, whether you know it or not. Always wear a little red. The rest doesn't matter. But wear a little red, especially when you talk to him. And talk to him soon. And look at the world when you talk to him. Remember, you can stand between him and the world or you can stand with him in the world. Either way you are staying in or you are going out." Then Nadja leaned back, exhaled, and dropped her head slightly to indicate that the rush of insight, and the reading, were over.

"Bless you, miss." The woman was in tears, dabbing at her eyes with a cotton handkerchief that she'd pulled from her purse. It was discoloring rapidly from her flowing mascara. "How much…I can't, I could never pay you enough…"

"Ten dollars is what most people leave as an offering. It's up to you. If this has been helpful…"

The woman rummaged in her purse and brought up a ten and a five. "Bless you, miss," she said again, as she shoved the two bills into the donation tray. And she got up to leave.

"Your plate, ma'am," Nadja reminded her.

"Oh, my lord, yes." The woman reached for it, looked at it a moment before putting it back into her purse. "Maybe I won't wash it," she said. "Maybe I'll just frame it, or spray it with that fix-it stuff. You know which stuff I mean? It's transparent."

Nadja smiled; the woman took it for approval of her plans, and hurried off.

Nadja inhaled deeply. She put her hands on her belly and exhaled. She got up from her chair, crossed to the door of the tent, and looked out at the gathering line, at the people waiting to see her. The man at the front of the line had health problems. Anyone could see that. Judging from his shape, it would be another plate with gravy stains.

"Who's next?"

. . .

Nadja is dancing in her sleep. Dancing alone at first. Dancing in a valley, surrounded by hills; her dance follows the curve of the hills, the once-liquid hills now cooled into ripples. She bends and turns, and her gaze takes them in. She feels them inside her, flowing in their origin, the power of hot lava spreading over earth. An old farmer steps up. May I cut in, he asks. Nadja, surprised, nods. Now they

*dance together, and he's easy to follow. Simple and old-
fashioned in his step. She's close enough to see his grizzled
beard, far enough from his face to not feel it. Who is this
man? He feels familiar, but she knows no farmers. His
countenance is sad and distant. When she looks at him
he looks away shyly, embarrassed to be caught looking
back at her. She wants to ask him who he is but when she
thinks the question something tightens up inside her and
fear walks in. She concentrates on the dance now, but is
distracted by his callused hand at the small of her back.
It's a sad, heavy hand. Why is she crying now? She closes
her eyes to regain composure, opens them to see her tears
on his face, too. He is looking over her right shoulder at
something in the hills. She tries to turn, arrange their dance
so she can see what it is, but he has become rigid, and
will dance only in place, with his gaze fixed on the distant curve of the hills. Nadja stops, and he clutches: the
hand at her waist encircles it, the hand holding hers clamps
down. Nadja is caught by this sad-faced, sad-handed
farmer. Who are you? She forces herself to ask the question, and when he looks away from the hills and directly
into her eyes she hears the answer in her bone marrow.
I am your name, he says silently. You are my grief.*

. . .

Helen stood on her front porch and watched the man she
called Harley spread manure in the east field. The wind, oblig-
ing on this day, carried the pungent odor of mint to her from the
acres that he'd planted two years ago. Some days, the wind would
shift and bring the scent of the chemical factory to the south, a
sweetish thick abrasive kind of smell. Sometimes it would bring
the yeasty warm smells of the bakery at the edge of town.
Between them, Heaven's Bread and Hoosier Chemical Company
employed about eighty per cent of Heaven's employable

citizens. Some worked on farms all summer and augmented their income by taking on a shift at Hoosier's during the winter.

They'd been lucky, Helen thought, that she'd managed this farm well enough that nobody who'd ever worked it had faced the necessity of taking a second job just to make ends meet. When Lester first came back from the war in '45, he'd made a halfhearted attempt to take on the business end, but Pops and Helen were doing it so well, it hardly seemed worth it. Then when Pops got killed, Helen just naturally kept doing what she did so well to begin with. A good thing, too, with Lester gone all these years. Besides, he never was any good at numbers.

His talent had been sensing what and when to plant. It was a talent Harley shared, so Helen allowed Harley to make those kinds of decisions. Like the mint. Mint was generally grown further up, where the soil was mucky. But there was one place by the creek where mint just flourished. So he put in a whole three acres and Helen sold it all to a tiny specialty tea company. Yes, Harley's timing with crops was perfect. He managed to have a lot in corn the years corn did well in Indiana and poorly elsewhere, and he suggested selling most of the cattle and putting over half the acreage in high-quality soybeans the very year the hippies started to appear in Indiana, rejecting red meat and baths, and generally giving their parents hissy fits. There were no hippies in Heaven, but Helen had found a small health-food processor up by South Bend who was willing to pay top dollar for all the pesticide-free soybeans Harley could produce. He'd kept all the pigs, though, the chickens, and a milk cow.

Helen had a network of friends who bought their fresh eggs and whole milk. Typically organized, she had arranged it so each of six customers came one day a week, Monday through Saturday. Minnie took most of Sunday's milk, and in exchange for the buttermilk which she just about lived on she provided Helen and Lester with butter in which to fry the dozen or so eggs that they kept each week. Minnie had grown up on a dairy farm, and had a little eight-quart butter churn — electric —

left over from when her folks died and the place had been auctioned off to that real estate man from Indianapolis.

Almost a decade had passed now since Helen's breakdown. Lester was still sleeping on the sofa bed in the den downstairs. After making a few attempts to draw his wife out about their shared past, he had given up. In conversation Helen tenaciously clung to topics that avoided the personal. The price of soybeans, the cure for udder sores on Jesse the cow, the news from church: who was ill with what this week, whose son or daughter was off to which job or college, who was expecting, whether it would rain, snow, sleet, hail, shine or ice up tomorrow. When, as Harley, Lester once asked Helen what her husband had been like, Helen snapped that it was none of his business and if he wanted to keep his job he would keep those sorts of questions to himself.

. . .

Lester met Annie Canfield the day Neil Armstrong walked on the moon. He had gone to take some pigs to market. On his way back, he stopped in at the carnival over outside Hartford City, and that was where he ran into Annie. She was half Lester's age, not quite twenty-five to his just-turned fifty, but a woman who had, as they say in covert tones, been through a lot. She started out with one strike against her when her father was counted among the casualties at Omaha Beach on D-Day the same month as her birth. Her mother took it hard, then finally remarried a fellow from Cincinnati when Annie was twelve. There was always some kind of bad feeling between Annie and her stepdad, and a couple years later when her mother said they were moving, Annie stayed behind at her married sister's to finish high school. Then she met Clarence. Nobody who knew him ever had an unkind word as such for Clarence. He was bright, polite, a hard worker, didn't drink or smoke, a churchgoer whose father was a preacher. "But think of what it would put kids through," people said, "to have a colored daddy." (She did want kids, didn't she?) Some remembered back in 1960 when Deanna Stoddard had to leave the state to get married. She went up to Chicago, they recalled, because in those days, colored and white couldn't legally get married in the state of Indiana. And that was where she died, too, they noted, when she hit that patch of ice on the Outer Drive. "It was on that funny bend, you know. Road builders up there ought to take a look at how we do it here. A straight road's always safer than one with a bend in it."

After Clarence's sudden departure for the West Coast, most folks thought Annie was, frankly speaking, better off.

Annie wasn't very patient with these opinions, or with the people who held them. She told quite a few of them to go to hell. Lester had heard the stories at Clara's Kitchen from Maurice and Bobby, who pointed her out one day as she walked by the café window.

"So that's Frank Canfield's baby," Lester said.

"Yep," said Bobby. "All growed up with her butt in trouble and her nose in the air."

She was at the carnival at the insistence of her sister, who felt a little fun might get Annie back on her feet again. Somehow separated from her guardian sibling and guide, Annie was wandering past the shooting gallery looking lost as Adam's off-ox when she bumped into Lester.

"Excuse me," Annie muttered, and when Lester said "No, excuse me. I just wasn't watching where I was going," Annie began to cry. It was just kind of like the hurt of the past two years rose up in liquid form and started to pour out, triggered by the unexpected graciousness in Lester's voice.

"Now, now, now," Lester said, with some alarm in his voice. "It surely can't be that bad."

Annie struggled to compose herself. Lester looked around the fairgrounds for an inspiration.

"Something is surely on your mind, little lady." He put a fatherly arm around her shoulder. "You know what I'm going to do? I'm going to treat you to having your fortune told. And I bet you it's going to be a good one, because I can see that you're about due for something wonderful to happen in your life."

Annie looked blankly at Lester. "Do I know you?" she asked.

"I knew your daddy," Lester said. "He was a good man. A good man. I'm Lester Breck. Come on. Let's get you a good fortune to cheer you up." He led the way to the fortune-teller's tent, where a woman in large earrings, a purple turban, and extravagant make-up sat at a small table. Annie, embarrassed, hung back. "Tell you what," Lester said. "You stay right here by the cotton candy. I'll go see how long a wait it'd be."

Lester planted Annie by the cart and walked over to the woman at the table. "How long a wait to get a fortune told?" Lester asked.

"I can tell you your fortune right now," the woman replied.

"Oh yeah?"

"If you've got ten bucks, my crystal ball says you can get laid within the next ten minutes."

"Never mind," he told the woman. He crossed back to Annie. "Forget the fortune," he said. "Let's get some cotton candy and go for a ride on the Ferris wheel. You know the very first Ferris wheel was over two hundred feet high? Made by a fellow named Ferris for the Chicago World's Fair."

• • •

Once Lester broke his marriage vows and slept with Annie, it just kind of let something loose in him. Ten years had been a long time to go without physical companionship. The affair with Annie was sweet and good and brief. It rekindled his interest in sex and hers in life. Temperamentally, though, Lester and Annie weren't much of a match. After a month or two, his deferential manner irritated her; her brashness embarrassed him. They went on to new lovers, without rancor, and when they ran into each other at the Blackford County Fair the next fall they even got together again, just once for old time's sake.

Of course, carrying on in Heaven proper was out of the question. Lester didn't want to hurt Helen, and he certainly wasn't looking for any big changes in his life. He just liked having sex again. So he generally made his contacts on the midways — usually by locating a sad-looking single woman in her thirties and offering to win a stuffed animal at the shooting gallery for her. If the carnival was too near home for comfort, he would take his lady friend to the Howard Johnson's in Muncie.

None of these liaisons lasted, but they helped Lester through some otherwise lonesome years. Since he was only a hired hand, Helen didn't even ask him what he did after working hours, on his own time. Lester was more than a little relieved about that.

Still, he missed Helen. They used to have such good times together. Even with the occasional romance, if it hadn't been for Stella's steady and sympathetic ear down at Clara's Kitchen, he might have gotten pretty depressed.

1 9 7 0

. . . .

THEY ALWAYS DID SAY TROUBLE comes in threes, and now Ellie knew why. First, her Grandpa Lawrence had a stroke on Lincoln's Birthday. They did what they could at County Hospital to get him through the initial crisis, but after a while he wasn't really getting any better, so they just sent him home. Reba set him up in a rented hospital bed in the front room so he could watch the Gillette Cavalcade of Sports and keep up with Huntley-Brinkley. It troubled Lawrence not to be able to talk clearly, and consequently he spent the better part of his waking hours in a foul mood.

Then Robert was sent home from the Vets Hospital too. The doctor thought that he and Lawrence should have some time together before Lawrence's obviously inevitable death. In retrospect it may not have been the best idea. Now that Robert was free from the supervision at Veterans, the little nips he had managed to smuggle into the hospital bloomed to a full return of constant inebriation. Even so, he was calmer now, probably as a result of the shock treatments, and maybe that is why the women of the household went on holding things together without noticing how badly he was deteriorating. Or perhaps they were simply too tired to care.

And Kathleen, in addition to battling constant fatigue, was distracted by a hard growing presence in her left breast. She tried to beat her troubles the way she always had — by keeping them to herself. She willed herself up in the morning, insisted herself through the day. So she surprised everyone by collapsing the morning of July 5 while getting ready for work. By then, the cancer had spread to her liver and spine. Now, no amount of determination was sufficient to get her out of bed. The house at 319 Elm Street became a full-blown hospital ward.

During these awful months, Ellie got a job at Clara's Kitchen to help make ends meet. Over summer break, she worked the lunch and dinner shifts; when school started up again, she just worked dinners. The fellows all knew what a struggle it was, and whenever possible left a tip for her, even though it was not the usual custom at Clara's.

September took Robert with it. Officially, it was an accidental drowning. Ellie found him in the tub the morning of the twenty-ninth. He'd long since given up the nicety of drinking from a glass. His bourbon bottle bobbed next to him. Ellie stood in the doorway looking for a long time before she called in sick to school and woke her grandmother. She tried to make out the floating figure as her father, tried to feel a connection. All she could think of, or feel, was that it would have saved a great deal of pain if he had never come back from Korea. Never married her mother. Never fathered her. She didn't feel guilty about this, only empty. Or rather, full of something very insubstantial.

They moved Kathleen to County Hospital right after Robert's funeral. Eunice Switzer came over twice a week to watch Lawrence so Ellie and Reba could drive out to see Kathleen. Most times, she was asleep. They hated to wake her, knowing what pain she was in, so they mostly sat by her bed and read. Reba passed the time looking through copies of the *Reader's Digest* from the waiting room. Ellie pulled a book off a shelf in the little library and found herself reading poems about Death by someone named Emily Dickinson. They weren't *all* about Death, but those were the ones that interested her the most. There was something comforting to her in the poet's ability to make even her mother's wasting illness sound beautiful and important.

She especially liked the line about Death being a dialogue between the spirit and the dust. That was how she felt. Like her whole life was a dialogue between the spirit and the dust.

By the time Kathleen died, two days before Halloween, Ellie had grown so fond of Emily Dickinson that she committed the one and only theft of her life. She took the book home with her.

When a second massive stroke took Lawrence, the day after Thanksgiving, Ellie was so numb that nothing seemed to matter. Now it seemed to her that dust had definitely had the last word. Stella even said to her, "You don't seem to be taking this one so hard. Didn't you and your grandpa get along?"

. . .

Sue Ellen Sue grew to be quite a good-looking young woman. She kept herself in shape so she could do all the strenuous routines involved in being a cheerleader. She kept working on hair — her own, her mother's, her sister's — learning how to cut and curl, and she kept up her diary.

> *Denny finally asked me to the Prom. We almost broke up last week because I wouldn't go all the way with him and he called Karen Brubecker and asked her to see True Grit with him. Shelley heard that he told Jerry he didn't want to be the only one at the Prom not getting any. So Shelley goes up to Denny and asks him right to his face if he's asking me to the Prom. And I guess he kind of didn't answer her straight out, so she asked him if it was true what she heard that he was planning to ask Karen. And she told him he was to be careful what he did with her because she heard Karen had to go to the doctor all the way down in Muncie because she had some kind of infection she didn't want anyone to know about. That she got from Sam's cousin Terry who's in Vietnam now.*
> *Shelley's not afraid to talk to a guy like that.*
> *I wouldn't have the nerve.*
> *But anyway, that night Denny calls me and asks me*

to go. So I said yes. So now I have to find a dress. Mom's going to take me down to Ayre's to find something. I don't want to get anything that's in the stores around here. They're just so icky.

I'm going to do my hair in ringlet curls, sort of piled on top with curls coming out like a pony tail in the back, only with a rhinestone-covered barrette to hold it up. And Shelley's I'm going to do like the hairdo in Seventeen this month for the medium-short hair and square face, because her face is more square than anything else.

But I just think it's cool that I'm going to do the Prom Queen's hair. Her attendants are all going to Michael's in Fort Wayne but Shelley had her hair done there last year when she went to the Prom at Northside with Chester Fullerton and she said he's really not as good as me.

Ellie wasn't on the bus again today. I heard she might have to drop out of school to help take care of her grandma. That's so awful — to have three people in your house all die practically at the same time. Nobody even knew her mom had cancer until it was spread all over I guess.

It scares me to even think about cancer. I'm glad I come from a long-lived family. Except Grandpa Amos, but that was an accident. He probably would have lived for a long time too if he hadn't gotten stuck on the tracks.

I think it's so cool that the Prom is going to last all night. I mean, it makes sense. When you spend all this time and money getting ready for it, you want it to last as long as possible.

I really like Denny. I think I might love him.

I think I'm going to tell everyone to call me Esse — pronounced Essie — as a nickname. Sue Ellen Sue sounds so silly. Esse is like based on my initials, but it's also like in Latin class the word for being. So it's like Esse Esse. I Am Sue Ellen Sue.

WHAT GRIEF, GUILT AND FEAR HAD ENGENDERED, jealousy finally put a stop to, in no uncertain terms. Here's how that happened. One day Helen was in Herman's Market deciding whether to buy one or two boxes of Cope's Dried Corn. It sat next to the split peas and kidney beans in the back corner of the far left aisle. That's not where Lester expected Helen to be. He expected her to be at the five-and-dime, picking up some new dish towels. But they were having a sale on dish towels at the five-and-dime, so instead of taking time to determine the best bargain, Helen had snatched up the last package of three priced-to-sell flour-sack towels and then decided to use the extra minutes to run over to Herman's for the corn. She wanted to try that recipe for corn custard that Minnie had raved about. The recipe was right on the box; Helen stood in the back of the store reading it to see how much she'd need to make a respectable-size dish for the church supper that was coming up in just a week.

Meanwhile, Lester had run into Maurice outside Herman's, and walked along with him through the store while Maurice picked up provisions for the week ahead. Since the divorce, he mostly ate Stagg Canned Chili, Armour Beef Stew, and Chef Boyardee Spaghetti-O's for dinner. These items were all in the next aisle over from the dried corn.

How could either of them possibly have known there was anyone else in that part of the store? It was the quiet time of day, and there surely didn't seem to be a soul anywhere near. So Maurice thought it was safe to rib Lester just a little.

"Say, Les," Maurice said, quietly and carefully, in the voice he probably hadn't used since eleventh grade when he and Lester competed to see who would get laid first, and compared notes on progress toward this goal at the back of their American Government class. Helen's ears pricked up. She knew the sound of a secret about to be told when she heard it. Maurice continued. "Saw your old Buick over to the Howard Johnson's down past Muncie last week. That little lady sitting in the front seat was quite a looker."

"I'd appreciate it," Lester replied, "if you'd figure that was someone else's car you saw."

"Don't worry, ol' buddy. Gotcha covered. What was she, about twenty? Twenty-one?"

"She's older'n she looks," was all Lester was willing to say.

"Well, she sure was a looker."

"You alone?"

"Now?"

"'Course not now. When you saw someone else's car that looked like mine."

"Oh, yeah."

"Well now, what were you doing at the motel?"

"Just stopped there for coffee and a hot dog. I like those buns they got, you know, like two pieces of bread hooked together. I like that better'n those rounded ones. On my way back from putting in an application down there at the glass factory."

"Is that a fact?" Lester welcomed the chance to change the subject. "You looking for something new?"

"Well, they say they might be closing down the bakery. Not right away, but I don't expect it's going to last much past Christmas. Hard to compete with the big guys, you know? Dick Kruger says the money they'd have to put into new equipment just doesn't appear to be worth it."

The next aisle over, Helen decided she'd stick with a Jell-O salad, put the corn back on the shelf, and walked as quickly as she could without looking like she was in a hurry out the store and back catty-corner across Main Street to the five-and-dime, where, moments later, an unsuspecting Lester found her waiting.

She kept quiet all the way home. She always did keep pretty quiet, so that didn't raise any alarm to Lester.

She waited until after supper. Until after he went out to turn the lights out in the chicken coop. When he stepped back into the house, Helen looked at him in astonished rage. "Where have you been, Lester Breck?"

At first Lester didn't register the significance of her outburst. "Why, out to the chicken coop," he said.

"For twelve years?" Helen demanded.

Lester couldn't do much but stand there with his mouth hanging open.

Helen went on, "What in the world possessed you to walk off like that? We're lucky Harley was around, or we probably would have lost the farm for sure."

"Who's Harley?" Lester dared to ask.

"Never you mind," Helen cut him off. "He's gone now, and you're back, so that's all that matters."

Praise the Lord, Lester thought, she's finally snapped out of it.

Now the truth of it was, Helen had snapped out of it pretty much right after she'd snapped into it, back in '60. But since Lester had been so willing to let it ride, she had decided there were some advantages to letting everyone think she was a little touched. Biggest among them was the excuse not to have sex. But now the need for that particular kind of distance was drawing to an end. She was pretty sure she was all the way through the change. The dread of another pregnancy that had haunted her ever since 1954 was finally easing up. And realizing that the man she so loved had finally sought companionship elsewhere opened her eyes to the fact that she could lose his affections forever, especially if she never returned them.

She didn't want to seem sex-crazy, though, so the only move she made was to return the sofa bed to its primary function.

Lester watched her pull the sheets from the bed he'd slept on for so long, fold the frame back, and put the cushions in place. Something close to hope fluttered in his chest. She was a mystery to him. Always had been. He'd always kind of liked that.

A FALL DAY IN HEAVEN holds the promise of a new year in the leaf smoke, a smell like spiced cider, a certain apple-crispness in the air, a "nip," as Winnie the Weather Girl used to say. Ellie pulled her heavy sweater, a bulky-knit white cardigan, over her crinkly black waitress uniform and hurried up the street to Clara's. Since she dropped out of school the year everyone but she and Grandma Reba died, she missed it. At least, she missed the excitement of the annual pilgrimage for school supplies and one new back-to-school outfit. The outfit would be too hot to wear the opening day of school, but she would wear it anyway, then put it in the closet until an October day like this one. The sweater she now wore was her last such purchase, made some four years before.

She rounded the corner and started up Main Street to Clara's. She was switching to breakfast shift, and it was her new task to start four pots of coffee before Stella opened the doors at six o'clock. No one much came in until seven or so, but Stella liked to be open anyway, for the occasional farmer grabbing a thermos-full on his way to a market, or a traveling salesman anxious to get an early start. But today there was already a customer. Stella had let him in to wait for his coffee. He sat at the counter, leaning on his elbows, chin cupped in his big-knuckled, workworn hands.

"Am I late?" Ellie asked anxiously.

"Naw, I just let Les in to set till we open," Stella said.

She followed Ellie to the kitchen and spoke quietly, conspiratorially. "Be nice to him, El. He's the one we're always talking about. Wife's a little crazy. Give him a sweet roll or something...on the house."

"Is she the one that comes in once a month to Seese's to get her hair done up in that fifties roll thing?"

"That's Helen Breck." Stella winked at Ellie and whispered, "Crazy as a bat," then felt compelled to add, "'course, she's been through a lot. Lost her only daughter really sudden back in '54. Right during the Centennial. It was an awful shock. There's more to it that I'll tell you soon as Lester leaves. And too, she was the one who found Charlene." Then she inhaled as if readying herself for a deep dive and strode out through the swinging doors to flip her sign from Closed to Open, to welcome a new day's business. "How's Helen," she called to Lester over her shoulder as she unlocked the door.

"Oh, prit near the same," Lester allowed. "She's got me out in the barn, you know." Lester knew perfectly well that everybody in town knew he'd been kicked out of the house, but protocol demanded that anyone talking to him feign ignorance and allow Les to frame it his way.

"What's that about? She think you're Harley again?"

"Oh, no. Long as she thought I was the hired hand, you know, she put me up in the spare room. No, now, see, she's decided that she's mad as heck at me for being gone all those years." Lester indulged in a childhood habit and crossed his fingers behind his back. He was leaving out just a little bit of the story. The part about how even though they'd been sleeping together again, the sex was no longer very satisfying, so he'd dared to stray once more from his marriage vows. And had been caught.

Helen's precise words to him as she ordered him to sleep in the barn had actually been, "Anyone with a dumb animal's sense of morality should just go on and sleep with them. Don't you touch me." He didn't exactly mean to fib about what she

62

said, but some things you just don't talk about with folks, and this was one of them.

"Why doncha take her up there to the hospital, Les?"

"Well, it don't hurt me none to go along with her. Shoot. I couldn't run the farm if she was in the hospital. She's terrific with the numbers. I was never good at any of that part of the business. Naw," he continued, with a bit of amusement in his voice, "I'll just fix up a little space out there. Pigs is actually pretty clean, you know. Heck of a sight better'n chickens, I'll tell ya that one thing for sure." And he crinkled his eyes and smiled a little. "I am gonna get me a little heater, though, down at the Plaza, I seen they had 'em on sale. It's getting a bit nippy out there at night." A little sad shadow flickered across Lester's face, and then it was gone again. "Say, did I ever tell you the one about the prize pig and the bantie rooster?"

By the time he left for the sale, it was nine o'clock. Learning Ellie's name, he had surprised her by saying how sorry he had been to hear about her mama, daddy and grandpa. Especially her daddy, he said, who had really never gotten over being in Korea. Ellie was intrigued.

"How well did you know him," she asked.

Lester said, "Oh, we drank a few beers together from time to time over at Pete's Gate. Back before he went into the hospital that last time. No, not well, but well enough to know he was one of those fellows who shouldn'ta gone to war. "I seen 'em like that in the big war, too," Lester said. "Nice fellows, but just something in 'em that snapped when they had to kill people. Or when they lost a buddy."

"Did you kill people?" Ellie stopped wiping the counter and watched Lester answer.

"I was pretty lucky," he said slowly, staring into midspace at some private scenario. "I never had to shoot once I got out of basic training. But I knew a lot of fellows who did. It wasn't easy for them, I can tell you that, too. But I don't reckon we had much choice. Tell you the truth, I don't know what I'da done with this here Vietnam thing. Seems to me they beat us over there, but don't seem like it has much to do with us, you know what I mean? 'Cept now we got all these boat folks comin' over. Say, Stell, did I tell you about the Laotian fellow the Ellis's cousins were sponsoring over in Columbus? Got arrested for shooting squirrels in the city park! Guess he thought that was how you hunt your dinner up here. Chuck said he was just about as mortified as could be. Judge told him, 'You're in America now. You better start buying your supper at the supermarket like everybody else!'"

When Lester left, Stella turned to Ellie and pronounced her judgment. "There goes one of the nicest fellows you could ever hope to meet. I hope he outlives his crazy wife so's he gets a few years of peace for himself before he dies. Heck," she grinned, "if something happened to Helen I'd be glad to take him in. He's pretty handsome for a man over fifty, don't you think? Sort of like Cary Grant? 'Course, I suppose Walter would object."

"Is he still alive?"

"Walter? To tell you the truth, I wonder about that sometimes. Since he got laid off, he doesn't seem to move much."

"Cary Grant."

"Oh, Cary! Why, sure he is. At least I think he is."

Ellie looked out the front window, where Lester had stopped to have a word with Bobby before climbing into his pickup.

"Where does he live?"

"Why, in Hollywood, I imagine," said Stella, and Ellie smiled, allowing Stella her jokes.

"No, I mean Lester."

"Oh, out about a mile past the fairgrounds. That big old farmhouse on Millstone that sits at the end of that long driveway right near the crossroads."

"Funny, I never met him before."

"Well, that's not too surprising." Stella grinned. "He was dead a dozen years."

"Lester Breck." Ellie was still watching him as he climbed into the truck and nodded good-bye to Bobby. Stella chortled. "Lester and Helen. Just about the oddest couple you'll ever find around here. Leastwise I hope so."

"I hope he comes in again sometime. He's kind of fun."

"Oh, he'll be in. He always comes in during the winter to get his coffee. Helen never could make a decent cup of coffee. You stay on the morning shift, you'll see him again."

. . . .

"HELEN PUT LESTER BACK OUT IN THE BARN. Caught him with that Forbalder woman. You know the one I mean. Edith's granddaughter. Lives over there in Gas City. Caught him with his you-know-what down." Minnie gossiped as deftly as Seese trimmed hair and wound curlers.

"Don't you mean up?" Seese liked to tease Minnie, who was still capable of blushing even through her prodigious rouge.

"Hush, now. You know what I mean. Caught him practically in the act. He was down at the state fair and didn't know Helen and I had come down too. I was looking at the limas when she saw them over behind the livestock pens with their hands all over each other. Then I guess they headed off to Lester's truck and that's where she caught 'em. Put him right out in the pigsty."

"And he let her do that?" Seese looked straight into Minnie's eyes through the big mirror they both faced.

"Oh, my, yes. Well, you know, Lester never did argue back with Helen. He never did contradict her. I used to think he was a real gentleman. Now I think maybe he just doesn't have the gumption to stand up for himself. I mean, look at the way he just hikes himself out there whenever she tells him. He's been in and out of that barn so many times it makes a person's head spin to hear about it. But she feeds him. Cooks his meals hot and takes 'em out to him, and brings him clean clothes and does his laundry and dishes."

"Well, 'course I never knew her before, 'cause it was the year I was born, but my grandma told me Helen hasn't really been the same since they lost their daughter." Seese astonished everybody with her ability to have learned and catalogued every item of interest in Heaven's history that any living customer might have been acquainted with. It was her personal imperative to be the most informed woman in Hutter County.

Minnie nodded. "Oh, that was hard on her. And to know there was a grandchild somewhere and not be able to find it. That just about broke her heart. Never even knew if it was a boy or girl." Minnie shook her head sadly at the injustice.

"Never even knew."

"Well, that just goes to show you."

"Yes, it sure does."

"Don't take too much off the top."

"Don't you worry."

. . . .

GRANDMA REBA GOT SICK IN JANUARY. Got the flu, and never got over it. The flu turned to pneumonia, and the pneumonia just hung on like the devil, making Reba weaker and weaker. Then on top of it all her heart started acting up.

Early in March, Ellie moved her bed into Reba's bedroom so she could hear her breathing at night. Reba was given to coughing spells that just about wore her out; Ellie finally convinced her to take the medication the young Dr. Hanson gave her to let her sleep. Doc Brubecker was retired now, and Reba didn't actually trust this new fellow, but she didn't have a whole lot of choice in the matter of doctors in Heaven, because the young Dr. Hanson was it.

Lying in her bed at night, Ellie could hear the freight trains passing by. They reminded her of the passenger trains that used to run through Heaven, back when she was a kid. And all the places she'd imagined. What had she been looking for in those faraway fantasy places? And the maps! Where are all those maps, she wondered.

She found them one day in June, in a dusty suitcase stuck up in the attic, and laid them out in order on her bedroom floor. With her bed gone, there was room for all of them: a map for each state, back from when maps at service stations were free, and you could get the entire set by writing to gas companies for your geography project.

Knee-deep in the quicksand of obligation that kept her in her hometown, Ellie began to look for Somewhere Else.

She began it as a diversion, and it turned into a meticulous and systematic search. Is this the only Heaven there is? she wondered first, and pored over her maps until she was convinced that the irony was indeed all hers. Though she did notice a Paradise in Pennsylvania, a Hell somewhere in Michigan, and a Purgatory in Maine.

She spent the better part of that summer and fall waiting for Grandma Reba to die, and analyzing her maps. Each item took some time to research. She wondered, for example, if it was just normalcy she craved. She found one Normal right in Indiana on the first day, but the others, in Kentucky, Alabama, and Illinois, took over a week to locate. If she wanted to be Happy, she found Texas, Arkansas, and Kentucky to choose from. For Revolution, North Carolina offered a possibility. She found Hope in twenty-four states; but was Hope what she really wanted? There was Love in five states, Grace in eleven, Faith in six and Charity in four. She found Heart in Arkansas. She found Win in Kentucky, then noted after an exhaustive search that there seemed to be no Lose or Draw anywhere. It's just as well, she thought. No Limbo...no Uncertainty...no Hate...no Dislike, even...no Questions and no Answers. She saw Fame — in West Virginia and Oklahoma. She discovered Rest in Kansas and Virginia. There didn't seem to be any Where, When, or How, but there was a Why in Arizona. And Glory? There were Glories in Georgia, Minnesota, and Texas. There were no fewer than eighteen Freedoms. She found Peace in Alabama, Wisdom in Kentucky, Missouri, and Montana. There was no place called Backwards, but there were two Forwards. I guess that's really it, she thought. Forward. I'd just like to feel like I'm going forward. So Ellie drew big red circles on her maps: one around Forward, Pennsylvania, the other around Forward, Wisconsin. But she stayed in Heaven, Indiana.

Meanwhile, the closer Reba got to death, the more her mind rode the roller-coaster tracks of her memory. Sometimes she was up — up at the crest and looking over some event, about to plunge fully into it. Sometimes she was down, exhausted, unable to see anything but the long slow pull ahead — the effort needed to draw her next breath, to swallow the next bit of food.

The past that Reba came to live in was a puzzle to Ellie. She hadn't paid much attention to her family as she was growing up, and had been especially impatient with the rambling stories her grandparents seemed so fond of. Now she was fascinated with the images that occupied Reba's mental landscape. Reba remembered all the way back to World War I. She remembered waiting for Lawrence to come home from the trenches.

"I wasn't in love with him then," she told Ellie one evening. "I was too young. But your great aunt Betsy was engaged to him. You see, Betsy and Lawrence graduated high school together in '14, when I was just thirteen. Then when Lawrence went off to France, Betsy would always read his letters out loud to me. Well, I started to feel like he was writing to me as much as he was writing to her. I'd write back, not anything serious, but just little chitchat to cheer him up. And then when they sent him back with shell shock, Betsy just didn't want to have much to do with him. She flew the coop and took up with Henry Cullum. Henry was color-blind, you see, so he never had to serve his time like Lawrence did."

"What was he like? I mean, what does shell shock do to a person?"

"Oh, he was awful jumpy at first. Somebody'd bang the screen door and he'd about have a fit. But he got over it, little by little."

"And you got married."

"June 5, 1921."

"And when was my dad born?"

"Well, now, that took a while. I miscarried three times in six years. And nearly did in '27, but I guess the Good Lord decided it was time for us to have a baby."

"But you never had any more?"

"No, never had any more."

"Because you didn't want any more?"

Reba shook her head. "No. I think the doctor did something to fix it so I wouldn't have any more. I never even had the curse after that."

Ellie had to smile. She tended to see it as a blessing.

Reba was worn out from her storytelling, so Ellie tucked her in.

On subsequent nights, she learned that Grandpa Lawrence had worked at Hoosier Chemicals, doing some kind of testing. Reba admitted that she never did know exactly what his job was. She revealed, under close questioning, that life after Robert was born had been difficult at first. Reba had been considerably weakened by the repeated pregnancies and even though her mother-in-law moved in with them to help out, the way Grandmama Lil and Lawrence got along made it almost more trouble than it was worth.

"When did Grandmama Lil die?" Ellie asked, astonished that this was a question that had never before occurred to her.

"Oh," said Reba, "not too long before you were born. 1952. She lived long enough to vote for Ike, and had a stroke just after Christmas that year. In fact, your mother'd just come home from the doctor's with the news that you were on the way and Lord, we were afraid she was going to lose you, too, the way she carried on. Oh, she and Grandmama Lil were just as close as could be. She was closer to Grandmama Lil than she was to her own family."

"And what did happen to her family? I mean I know they all moved to Atlanta after Mom and Dad were married, but why didn't they ever write or visit?"

"Well, you know your Grandma Flynn never recognized your mother's marriage, because it wasn't in the Catholic Church. And your dad didn't think much of Catholics. So there wasn't really too much love lost between your father and your mother's folks."

Because these exchanges exhausted Reba so much, Ellie was often left with questions that had to wait for a week or more to be asked. On these days, she would sit on the floor by

Reba's bed and read Emily Dickinson poems to her. Ellie's favorite was one about growing wings from reading a book. "What liberty a loosened spirit brings." Once, when she was sure Reba was sound asleep, she read that poem to her ten times in a row, and then repeated the last line another three times. Then cried, but she wasn't sure whether the tears that ran down her cheeks and dripped onto the thin pages of the poetry book were for Grandma Reba or herself.

There were great gaps in Reba's memory. Places she could not or would not go. Though World War I and the Depression were crystal-clear to her (she recalled such details as washing her floors with the old dishwater to save on soap), World War II was sketchy. And she had almost nothing to say about Robert past the age of twelve. When Ellie asked if he'd been a heavy drinker before the Korean War as well as after, Reba furrowed her brow and contended that she didn't remember him ever being a heavy drinker.

"Talk about repression!" Ellie commented to Stella one morning. She told Stella, too, about her restlessness and her map search. Stella smiled broadly.

"I've been to Brazil, Georgia, Peru, Russia, Cuba, Sweden, and China," she said, "and I never had to leave the state." She pointed out towns on an Indiana map she kept at the cash register for lost travelers. "Maybe you could do a few side trips first, and see if anything feels far enough away."

"I don't know," said Ellie. "To tell the truth, I don't know what I'd do anywhere else. All I know how to do is waitress."

"Well, people eat everywhere," said Stella. "'Course I'd miss you. But maybe just going down the road a piece would help. Think about it."

"I will," promised Ellie.

. . .

The dead in a small town have so much life. Their absences leave remarkable holes in the social fabric. Their recipes are missed at Christmastime. Their stories, repeated so often that everyone knows them, never sound quite the same with another one doing the telling: "Well, Lawrence used to say…" or "I remember your grandma would always tell about…." No, it just wasn't the same.

They become a living history of themselves in these retellings. Then too, after death is when their secrets come out. Attics have to be sorted through, basements need to be cleaned. If they are the last in a local line, it's a field day for the kind neighbors who help to sort, clean, and organize for the estate sale.

Eunice Switzer volunteered more than once to help Ellie after she was left alone in the big house on Elm Street, but Ellie carefully and politely declined the offers.

"Oh, we got most of that cleared out in '70," she would say, and '70 was, as everyone knew, the year Robert, Kathleen and Lawrence all died.

Eunice Switzer was just a few years younger than Grandma Reba. She'd watched the household closely into a fifth decade, ever since she and her husband Earnest moved in next door right after the big war.

A suspicious woman by nature, Eunice spent her life testing the veracity of her family and neighbors. She steamed open Earnest's mail, then resealed it and waited to see if he told her what she already knew it contained. When her three daughters were growing up, she bought diaries for each of them, then read every word they ever wrote in them. She knew which drinking glasses best conducted sound through walls. It was as if she were convinced that everyone else was conspiring to withhold the same secret — that life was somehow much more joyful and engaging than she found it to be, and that everyone but she knew why. Someday, with planning, luck, diligence, and the proper equipment, she would overhear that secret and everything would fall into place.

Eunice Switzer was the last person in Heaven to give up her party-line telephone. She had mastered the art of listening in without being detected; nevertheless, one by one, her neighbors opted for privacy. Finally, there'd been no one left on the line but the Switzers and Miles Dumbauld, who never talked to anyone anyway and didn't even call an ambulance to take him to the hospital the night he had his heart attack. Just sat on his porch and died, and that's where they found him three days later when they realized the newspapers had started to pile up. Eunice felt personally cheated out of being the first to know of Old Man Dumbauld's death. It sent her into a depression from which she never fully recovered.

Of course, you don't snoop on people for thirty-five years without them getting wind of it. Ellie knew all her life that Mrs. Switzer was a snoop. She'd practically been born under that watchful eye, peeking through the crack in her lace curtains. Growing up, Ellie had always been aware that any play on the east side of the house was recorded for posterity in the brain of the neighbor who stood at her kitchen sink, ostensibly washing dishes, to keep on eye on whatever the children decided to do in the back yard.

The border of sweet peas between the Switzers' house and their own couldn't have been more effective if it had been high-voltage wires. All the kids knew that any ball bouncing over that line never returned. They imagined the Switzers' basement filled bottom to top with confiscated balls, and they weren't too far from the truth.

Knowing that an attic window light would arouse interest, Ellie sorted through all the boxes by bringing them down to her second-floor bedroom. There was a stamp collection that had been her father's when he was a boy. She sold it to a dealer in Fort Wayne. There were stacks upon stacks of *Look* magazines. The county library said no, no value to them, so Ellie burned them, keeping just the one issue that had appeared the week of her birth.

Numerous trunks of clothing had already been discovered by squirrels and moths, and went directly to the dump. She kept a bit of faded, tattered lace from her mother's wedding gown, which otherwise was completely destroyed.

One box, in the back corner, contained ledgers. Seven dusty books, with no labels of any sort. Just dates, names, and numbers. In her grandfather Lawrence's careful handwriting, she saw lists of many of Heaven's oldest family names. After each name the sum of $10 was neatly written. The ledgers ran from 1922 to 1928. From a high of 483 names in 1927, the list dropped to a mere 27 in 1928. Tucked in the back of the 1924 ledger was a newspaper clipping, so brittle it broke at the touch. "Klan Pride in Heaven," said the headline. "Hundreds March in Display of Unity and Christian Values." In front, holding up the banner at the head of the parade, were two figures in Klan regalia — robes, hoods, crosses stitched on their chests. Behind the banner were line upon line of others, all hooded and robed. Along the sides, spectators lined the street. Ellie stared at the picture. There at the side of the parade route was her grandmother Reba — young, of course, with an oddly indecipherable expression on her face. Next to Reba, a tight-faced young woman stood with a hand on a little girl's shoulder. The girl, in turn, was holding hands with a younger brother. He had to be her brother, they looked so much alike. The children, maybe five or six years old, stared fearfully at the adults marching past them. Something about their faces caught her. She tossed most of the ledgers out, but she kept the one with that clipping.

. . .

After Ellie auctioned off the house and paid all the hospital and burial bills, she had just about enough money left to take a nice vacation somewhere, and certainly no one would have faulted her for doing so, but she wasn't quite sure where she would go. So she put the money in a savings account, forgot about it, and went back to work at Clara's Kitchen. She rented the little house from Stella, the one down the street from the restaurant. It just worked out that it was free, because when Hoosier Chemicals had another round of layoffs, the family that had lived there for so long packed up and moved on.

"You can have it cheap," Stella told her, "if you don't mind fixing it up. I got too much on my hands to get to it right now."

Painting the place would give Ellie something to do. It was good for her to keep busy, Stella thought. Keeping busy was Stella's life. She had an apprehension that if she ever stopped being busy, the walls of her world might crumble. And if it was good for her to keep busy, she reasoned, it was good for everybody.

Ellie didn't bring much with her. The large dark chifforobes, sideboards, chests, and bureaus that had dominated her grandparents' home all went to Zucker, the secondhand dealer out on Route 26. She kept just one small trunk from her past. It contained a set of miniature ceramic horses, collected when she was nine; her maps; a few books, including *Heidi* and the book of Emily Dickinson poetry; the yearbook from her junior year in high school; the scrap of wedding lace; and the dusty ledger, with the picture of Reba Denson and the solemn children watching the parade.

When she passed by the house she grew up in, she saw young children playing in the yard and a tired-looking woman lifting her bony arms to hang out wash, or sweeping dust from the porch, or calling the children in to eat — she imagined tomato soup and grilled-cheese sandwiches. The realtor who bought it had covered the outside with yellow vinyl siding, and it now seemed as if the house of Ellie's childhood had simply vanished from the face of the earth.

What she liked about Stella's little place was that it was full of nooks and crannies. There were built-in bookcases, little ledges, and cupboards everywhere. She painted the walls pale green, with antique white for the woodwork, shelves, and doors.

After she finished painting the upstairs, she had a half gallon of white paint left, so she took it to the basement and regarded the immense pantry shelves that stood against the east wall.

She was completely unprepared for what happened when she pulled the shelves away from the wall in order to paint the back edge. The whole arrangement swung out smoothly, like a huge door, revealing a dirt chamber about six feet by four feet. At the back of the chamber was a tunnel. Ellie couldn't see how far it went. She abandoned the painting and ran for a flashlight.

Carefully, she stepped into the tunnel; carefully, she eased her way on through the passageway. To test her courage, she turned the flashlight off for a second, but the pitch-black made her heart pound and she turned it back on. Her palms were sweaty and she had to keep wiping them on her pants in order to keep a grip on the flashlight. After several hundred yards, the beam of the flashlight picked up some dim shapes. Boxes, some large, some small; bottles, jugs, and enormous cans. When the light picked up the brand name on a huge can of chicken broth, Ellie laughed out loud. Now she knew she was in the basement storage area for Clara's Kitchen.

On her way back, she noticed a side tunnel. Feeling a bit braver now, she dared follow it. This tunnel ended abruptly beneath a set of floorboards. A small wooden ladder, covered in cobwebs, rested against the wall. Ellie tucked the flashlight in her pocket and climbed to the top. The boards over her head were wide and loose. She managed to balance on the ladder while she pried one up and shined the light through. There was Stella's van, and her garden tools hung neatly on the wall. Ellie was looking into the little garage on the alley behind Clara's Kitchen.

Something about her experience made Ellie want to keep it a secret. She climbed down, turned back, and quietly retraced her steps. She painted the shelves, pushed them back into place against the wall, and never let on to Stella that she knew about the secret passage.

"WELL, ONE OF MY GREAT-GRANDMAS WAS Sue Ellen and another one was Ellen Sue. Just one of those strange coincidences that happen sometimes. But anyway, they were both still alive when I was born, and I was the first great-grandchild for both of them. Sue Ellen was Daddy's grandma. She was a real pioneer-type lady. Big and strong, and used to working hard and getting her way." Seese was sitting in Clara's Kitchen having coffee with Lester, Walter, and an encyclopedia salesman. Minnie, who was permanently booked for the first Saturday-morning appointment of each month, was laid up with a bad cold, so Seese had an hour or so before she had to be back in her shop.

The fellow from Britannica had got her going, asking her where the name Seese came from. "It's not a name you usually hear."

That was all he had to say. Everybody but the salesman knew Seese was just about the only person in Heaven who could outtalk Lester. Lester winked at Stella and motioned to her to fill Seese's cup again. She brought a fresh pot over and filled the cups all around, then pulled up a chair next to her husband.

Seese glanced at Stella. "Thanks, Stell."

"Go on," Lester prompted. "Tell him."

"Well, now, Gram Sue Ellen let it be known that she wanted this baby — me — to be named after her. If I was a girl, which of course I was. But that was before I was even born. Now my mama didn't particularly like that name. Said it sounded too fluffy, like a feather. But Gram Sue Ellen wasn't any kind of fluffy. And if they weren't going to name me, if I was a girl, after her, she planned to die of aggravation and leave it on their consciences. So Mama pretty much had to give in, but she said if one great-grandma was to be honored, both ought to be. Gram Ellen Sue wasn't pushy about it the way Gram Sue Ellen was, but Mama said if Gram Ellen Sue got left out she might die from disappointment too, and she said Gram Ellen Sue deserved to outlive Gram Sue Ellen any day, anyway. So she prayed to have a boy and avoid the whole question and that's the way they left it till the morning I decided to come on into the world. If I had come out a boy, I'd have been Franklin Jeffrey. Franklin after Roosevelt, and Jeffrey after my mother's brother who was killed in a combine accident when he was twenty. He was one of those fearless types, I guess, and when his mother told him to be careful he'd just say who's afraid of machines? Well, he ended up in a bale of hay one day, at least a bunch of him did, enough so's they had to have a closed casket at the funeral."

"I remember Jeffrey," Lester said. "Terrible accident. That's how my daddy died, too, you know."

"Let her finish," Stella chided, pouring more coffee all around.

"But I came out a girl," Seese went on, "and that's when the ruckus began. My Daddy saying Sue Ellen, my Mama saying why not Ellen Sue? And it was old Doctor Brubecker's nurse, I guess, finally just said to call me Sue Ellen Sue and be done with it.

"I coulda done without that name growing up, I can tell you. You know how they call the pigs in to slop? Well, you know how many times I got called 'Sue Ellen Sooey?' More'n enough. It even happened once after I got my license and opened shop..." She turned parenthetically to Lester and Stella. "That A.J. Shaw, you know he was always the one who'd start that kind of stuff when we were young. Well," Seese went on, "he has the nerve to tell his little Danny to come up and ask me why don't I call it Sue Ellen Sooey's House of Hooey. I told him to tell his daddy he'd need more than a House of Beauty to put his face back together if I ever heard that again. Danny's just like A.J., you know. I didn't have to worry about scarin' him, talking too rough to him. I just had to make him know I meant business. I've worked too hard to get to where I am without some roughneck little monsters making fun of my name."

"Amen to that," Stella chimed in.

"They don't teach kids any kind of respect anymore."

"No, they sure don't."

"Well, anyway." Seese turned back to the salesman. "That's how I got my name. Like I said, I hated it when I was younger. So I thought to give myself a nickname. I figured Esse for the initials S, E, but everybody just kind of added it on and started calling me Sue Ellen Esse Sue. Then when I married Denny Ellis and became Sue Ellen Esse Sue Ellis, it was just too much. It was Lester here that decided to take the first initial of each name and call me Seese. And that just kind of stuck. So now I'm Seese.

"Now if I'd had girls I'd have named them names nobody ever had before. Something like Harmony, only change it somehow — like Harmona. Or if I'd had twin girls I would've called them Clarissandra and Marissandra. But for my boys I picked one-syllable names. I think that sounds stronger. Mel, Ned, Chip, and Sam. I like to make names be meaningful in some way. That's just the way I am. That's why I call it Sue Ellen Sue's House of Beauty instead of just Beauty Shop. See, there's a difference between a shop and a house."

"Les knows that, don't you Les?" Stella teased.

Lester looked at the clock. "What time did you say you have to be back in your shop?"

"Ten," said Seese.

"Well, it's just about five till now."

"Omigod. Don't tell me I talked for an hour straight."

"We won't mention it, will we, Stell?"

Seese ran out so fast she forgot to pay for her coffee. Lester started to pay for it, but Stella stopped him. "We can afford to treat once in a while," she said. "In exchange for a good story."

"Why, then, I should have a few free cups myself," said Lester. "Much talking as I do in here."

"I oughta charge you extra," Stella countered, "much listening as I do. But just to show you how nice I am, I'll give you a day-old doughnut and a free refill."

"I thought the refills was always free," said Walter, puzzled.

"They are."

"In that case," said the salesman, "I'll have another cup, too."

. . . .

STELLA'S CUSTOMERS WERE MOSTLY REGULARS, and the ones who weren't were usually salesmen on their way through from Millgrove to Montpelier or taking the scenic route from Hartford City to Liberty Center. A tiny old woman who looked like she could be anywhere from seventy to a hundred was out of the ordinary. Naturally, everyone took notice. She sat at the front table and ordered two cups of coffee, then walked to the cash register and asked for a phone book. Ellie hovered nearby, hoping it wasn't too obvious that she was reading upside down across the counter to try to see who this unusual customer was looking up. All Ellie could make out was that whoever it was, was on the Dawson–Furtwangler page.

The old woman returned to her table, where she was joined by another woman who'd just come in. Nobody recognized her, either: late twenties, early thirties, striking, on the thin side, but muscular, olive complexion, quick eyes that swept the place in a split second. Ellie brought water and menus, arriving in time to hear the younger woman ask, "Did you find any Densons?"

Everyone else in the place — which is to say, Stella, Bobby, Maurice, Pete, and Walter — suspended whatever they were doing and quietly listened up. They had better manners than to stare, but you can be sure they were keeping an ear on things.

"Just one. *E Denson.* Could be her. Could be parents. The phone book's a couple of years old. She might have moved or gotten married and have a different name now." To Ellie she said, "That soup of the day does look good, but we're just having coffee for now."

Ellie was having trouble finding her voice, so she wordlessly took up the menus and stood back from the table, acutely aware of the covert attention everyone was paying to the scene. Stella took the lead. "Looking for someone?" she asked from behind the counter, where she'd suddenly developed a need to rearrange salt and pepper shakers at the end closest to where the strangers were sitting.

"A woman about my age," said the younger of the two. "Named Ellie after Eleanor of Aquitaine. Ellie Denson was her name twenty years ago, and might could be still."

Stella thought Ellie was going to fall down. She sagged a little, and rocked unsteadily. "Oh my god" was about all she could manage to say. Then she said it again. Maurice and Bobby exchanged glances. Pete caught Walter's eye. Stella started out from behind the counter, ready to assist. Ellie said "Oh my god" a third time. Then she sat back against one of the counter stools so she wouldn't have to waste any energy doing anything other than taking a very close look at the two women at the table. "The swings?" she asked hesitantly. "The park? Nadja?"

The woman nodded, and broke out in a smile so big — well, if it had been any bigger there wouldn't have been room on her face for it. The old woman looked mighty pleased, too. Then Ellie did something people in Heaven don't do too much of. She held out her arms in a wild, wide gesture of welcome that invited, no, compelled Nadja to stand up and move into the hug. They clung to each other for quite a few seconds longer than is customary in central Indiana, but then, they had twenty-one years to cover in their embrace. Finally, the usual reserve of Hoosiers emerged, and they backed away from each other, a little embarrassed at having displayed so much open emotion in front of so many people.

Stella's instincts told her Ellie needed another break, even though she'd just finished her lunch. When Ellie protested that there were customers still to be served, Stella pointed out that they were all finished up anyway and about to leave. "Weren't you, boys?" And she maneuvered them past the cash register and out, on back to work. Then she insisted that Ellie and Nadja take the back booth and catch up on whatever it was they obviously needed to catch up on. She poured herself a cup of coffee, warmed Granny's cup as well, and sat down with her. She had her own reconnaissance mission to conduct, plus she welcomed a chance to chat with someone from the outside world.

In the back booth, Nadja explained their sudden return to Heaven. "Granny's daughter died," she said, "and Granny was the beneficiary of her life insurance. So she decided to retire."

"Your mother?" Ellie stirred a sugar cube into her coffee.

"Granny isn't my real grandmother," Nadja said. "I was sort of adopted. I don't know who my mother and father were."

"Oh." Ellie dropped her gaze to the coffee and stirred it some more, afraid that she'd intruded on private territory.

Nadja didn't seem to be annoyed. She continued her story. "It was a real surprise," she said, "because she hadn't seen Peggy for about fifteen years. They didn't really get along very well. Peggy ran away, kind of. When she was sixteen she married some fellow from Michigan to get away from the carnival, and I guess she hated Granny for not having some regular kind of job. She was married two or three times but she never had any kids herself. The last time Granny saw her — the only time I ever met her — was when her third husband died and she came to our winter house in Richmond after the funeral. She only stayed a couple of days. She and Granny had a big fight about something, and then she left. So all of a sudden Granny gets a letter from this lawyer in Ann Arbor saying Peggy died and left Granny $15,000. And Granny decided that eighty-six was old enough to retire. So we came here to find a house."

"Why here? I mean, I'm glad you're back, but it's not a place I'd think of choosing if I had the choice."

"Granny just said that she always liked this place. Ever since we came through here that year we were — nine, was it?"

Nadja smiled shyly at Ellie. "I liked the idea too. You were the only friend I ever really had outside the carnival. I was curious to see if you'd still be here."

"I'm still here," Ellie sighed.

Nadja watched Ellie stir another sugar cube into her cup. "I lost your address right after we were here in 1963. There was a blowdown and everything in our tent literally went flying away in the wind. Somewhere in Iowa. That's why I never wrote to you. We were going to write to each other, remember?"

Ellie remembered. She had waited all that fall, through the winter and on through the next summer for Nadja's promised letter. That was when she had given up hope that anyone or anything interesting would ever again come into her life in Heaven.

On the other side of the cafe, Granny sat consulting with Stella. Stella called over to Ellie, "Ell, is that little house still for sale? You know, the one behind Herman's Market?"

Ellie was surprised. "Yes," she said, "but isn't that the one they say is haunted?"

Stella's face took on a slow smile. "Nancy here says if a haint gets her a good price, she can live with it, and I believe she can."

. . .

Granny settled back in the shampooing chair and let her head nestle in the cold porcelain dip in the sink. She'd been asking around town for the story behind the haunt, and more than one person had recommended hearing it from Seese, who knew the story best. Besides, Granny considered having one's hair shampooed one of life's luxuries, and now that she was officially retired, she had decided she would indulge herself on a weekly basis. Seese was flattered that Granny had come to her. Not for the shampoo. She knew she had the only place in town for that. But for the history of her community. She drew herself up just a tiny bit taller than her regular five-foot, four inches, and launched into it.

"Here's the way I heard it. It was back during World War II — this woman Charlene came to town. Big woman but good-lookin'. Don't recall that anyone knew for sure where she came from, but she had a little bit of money, not a lot, mind you. I think she probably came up from Indianapolis. Well, anyway, she rented out the front part of Mrs. Lewis's house over there on First Street, and hung her shingle out to do haircuts and perms. 'Course she didn't do too well right at first, but then towards the end of the war, when all the men started coming home, business started booming. All the ladies getting gussied up to welcome their fellows back. That and the fact that Agnes Siebold finally retired. That's Artie Siebold's grandma. You know Artie Siebold at the bank? They say she must've been eighty by then. Said she felt she could stop working because there was finally someone who could take her place. 'Course, I guess some of Agnes's customers never would go to Charlene. They were just loyal to Agnes and that was all there was to it, so Agnes kept a chair in her back room. She did that till she died in…'53, I believe they said it was, just after Ike's inauguration. This is just what I heard, mind you. I was only a gleam in my Daddy's eye at the time. Is that too hard?"

Seese had realized that she was scrubbing Granny's head with a vigor that might be too much for the old woman. But Granny shook her head no, and Seese went on. "Well anyway, Charlene did real well — next thing everyone knew, she bought Agnes's old shop, and even hired old Miss Bickford to do shampoo and nails for her. 'Course, she wasn't old then. In fact, I guess in those days she was pretty young.

"Well, they say she worked long hours, Charlene did, opened at six in the morning some days for the folks who had to go to work by nine, and stayed open till seven at night on others for the ones who came after work at five. Then on Saturday she just did ten till two. And Sunday of course she was closed. Went over there to First Christian. Well, that's the way it went, oh I guess close to twenty-two years. Then in 1964 we had that big ice storm. Everybody was iced in for over a week. Now that I do remember, 'cause I was turning ten and my birthday party had to be canceled, after we bought all the cake and ice cream and balloons and everything. School was closed for a week, and we had to go almost till July to make up for it."

Seese paused for dramatic emphasis while she finished rinsing the shampoo out of Granny's hair and wrapped a big white towel around her head. "And when the thaw came and we started to get around a bit, that's when they found her. On the eighth of January. Elvis's birthday." Again, she paused, and pursed her lips as if the memory were her own as she led Granny back to the chair in front of the mirror where she would comb and dry her hair. "It was Helen Breck found her first, they say. She had a ten o'clock appointment and she got there 9:45 and wasn't no one there, so she waited, thinking, you know, maybe Charlene's street was still a little icy, but then when it came to be ten, and then 10:30, well, she knew something was wrong."

Seese had flicked the hairdryer on low, so the noise wouldn't be too loud to talk over. "Because Charlene never missed an appointment once — never in twenty-two years. So she called up to the police station and they went over to Charlene's house. You know, Cecil really let it get run down before he died. And it's stood empty so many years now. But Charlene kept it real nice, painted and all. And Harry — 'course, you wouldn't know Harry Hess, but he used to be on the police force. Retired the year I graduated, and moved down to Florida with his wife May about five years ago. He was on duty that day."

She flicked the dryer off, and began to comb Granny's hair out. It was long, fine, and nearly white. "Back up on the back of your head? Like you had it?"

Granny nodded to Seese's reflection in the mirror. Seese continued, "He came up the walk and he says he felt a chill. Not from the weather. Something different about it. He knocks and there's no answer. He knocks again. Same thing. So then he walks in the house — no one ever locked their doors in those days, you know. Everything all in place, neat and tidy as a pin — and he looks in the bedroom and there's no one there, and he looks in the kitchen and there's no one there. About that time, he hears a holler from Helen in the bathroom, so he looks in there and there she is — " she punctuated this by sticking a hairpin deftly into place, " — in her nightgown, dead on the floor. Looked like she'd collapsed while getting ready to take a bath, 'cause there was clean water in the tub." Another hairpin. "She looks real dead, and she's cold to the touch, but Harry's trained in lifesaving, you know, so he feels for her pulse." Another. "Doesn't feel anything." Two more, and Granny's hair is back in place. "Then he rolls her over so he can put his hand in front of her mouth — to see if he can feel any breathing — and that's when he notices. She's got five-o'clock shadow. Not just a little mustache. Lotsa women have a few little hairs on their upper lip. But Charlene's got a heavy growth of beard. And then the way Harry told it he hears Helen again and darned if she isn't screaming for real this time."

Seese handed Granny the hand mirror and spun the chair around so she could see how the back looked. She talked to the back of the hand mirror. "The fact of the matter is, rigor mortis has set in, and now that Charlene's turned over, Helen and Harry can't hardly believe their eyes, because Charlene's rigor mortis makes real clear something that not one person ever suspected in twenty-two years: Charlene is a man. A dead man, with the biggest erection you ever saw."

Granny lowered the mirror and looked at Seese.

"Well, not that you ever saw...I mean, not that I'm presuming what you've seen and haven't seen." A bit flustered, Seese took the mirror back and put it down.

"Now, when you think about all those secrets ladies tell their hairdressers, and how they all must have felt, realizing they'd been talking to a man all those years, thinking it was another woman — well, it just makes you wonder."

"Yes, it does," Granny affirmed. Seese hardly noticed that these were the first words Granny'd actually said since she entered the shop.

"The next ten years, anybody wanted a perm or a cut, they had to go on up to Fort Wayne or Marion or over to Hartford City. So when I got to finishing high school, they got the committee together and raised the money to give me my scholarship to beauty school down in Indianapolis — so's I could come back and reopen the shop. Charlene used to just call it Charlene's. I decided to call it Sue Ellen Sue's House of Beauty. I've done pretty well with it. The ladies here know who I am. They know I'm not going to surprise them. We don't need any more of those kinds of surprises around here. No, ma'am."

"No, I don't suppose you do," Granny nodded. And she thanked Seese, paid her, made an appointment for the same time the next week, and headed out to meet the realtor.

After Granny left, Seese realized she'd forgotten to tell her about how after Cecil Moser moved in he went crazy living in the little house, and how he died young of "natural causes," and how Maurice when he was still over at the bakery said he saw Charlene through the bathroom window plain as day when he stayed there late one night to do the inventory reports. She was walking back and forth with a big pair of scissors in her hands, just snipping. Snipping at the air.

· · ·

Nadja knew that she was a disappointment to Ellie. She could tell it from the way Ellie glanced around the living room of the little house and asked, "Did you get the chifforobe at Zucker's Second Hand?"

In fact, they'd gotten everything there: the faded brocade sofa and chair, their threadbare arms hidden by dark lace doilies, the heavy oak sideboard, the rocker with the nubby upholstery-like seat covering, the glass-door bookcase and the stained-glass floor lamp that Granny took such a shine to. "Yeah," Nadja confessed. "The stuff we had before was even more worn out, so we left it behind. I know this big stuff looks kind of silly in a little house, but Granny liked it because she said it would be impossible to move. It feels permanent, you know? Like we'll stay here a while."

"Where is Granny?" Ellie wondered. She'd almost told Nadja about how the chifforobe used to stand in her grandmother's bedroom, but when Nadja characterized the furnishings as worn-out and silly, Ellie suddenly felt embarrassed to acknowledge it. Everything in their conversation so far was feeling awkward, but she couldn't put her finger on the cause. She hoped a change of topic would dispel whatever it was.

"She's out of town for a couple of days," Nadja said. "She went down to Indianapolis to talk to some lawyers. She said she wants to get a will drawn up now that she has something to leave me."

"Why Indianapolis? There's a lawyer in Hutter County."

"Just her instinct for keeping her business private, even though she knows everyone else's." Nadja had a way of delivering a line totally deadpan, and then following it with the tiniest smile. "At least she will, by the time she gets back."

Ellie's expression made it clear she didn't understand.

"She went down there with Wilma Porter."

"The postmistress?" Ellie asked, feeling ignorant beyond redemption.

"She's going down to some postmasters' convention or something."

"I still don't get it."

"Who knows a town's business if not the postmistress?"

"But Wilma's pretty closemouthed."

"No one is closemouthed when Granny gets to them."

"Well, at any rate — " Ellie reached into her bag and held a large bottle aloft, "I brought some champagne to celebrate your being back in Heaven. And to christen your new home. Do you drink champagne?"

"When the occasion calls for it," Nadja said, "and I think this surely qualifies. But we'll have to drink it out of coffee cups. We don't have any wineglasses."

"No problem," Ellie assured her as she popped the cork and sent it ricocheting off a wall.

Nadja stepped into the kitchen and returned with two mugs, which Ellie filled to the top.

"Here's to your new home in Heaven," Ellie toasted.

"Here's to old friends," Nadja replied, and then, overcome by sudden shyness, each drank her portion down without a pause.

"So," said Ellie as she refilled the cups, "what have you been doing for twenty-one years?"

"Plates," Nadja said, and she told Ellie how under Granny's tutelage she had honed her skills in reading what people left behind when they ate. "But I don't want to do it anymore," she said. "People take it too seriously. I want to get a normal job. Here's to a normal job." Nadja raised her cup.

"Here's to whatever you want," said Ellie, raising hers.

"A normal job," repeated Nadja.

"Whatever," said Ellie. They settled into sipping, and the awkward silence between them returned. Ellie finally broke the quiet. "I should warn you, I'm a cheap drunk."

"Me, too."

Ellie smiled a tentative smile at Nadja and went back to sipping. Nadja followed suit. Ellie didn't know how much to say — how much she could say. "I've waited all this time for you to come back," she blurted out finally, then flushed.

Nadja looked at her in astonishment.

"I mean, I really liked you. I missed you. I always wondered about what you were doing. About all the exciting places you got to go to."

"Van Wert?" asked Nadja. "Columbia City? Toledo?"

"Well, you know, it's a start," said Ellie. "If you've been in one place all your life…"

"Sounds okay to me," said Nadja. "I'm ready to stay put for a little while, I think. At least Granny is, and I can't blame her. And she smiled that little smile.

"So," said Ellie, pouring their third cupfuls. "I've got another bottle of this stuff. Shall we get really plastered?"

"Why not?" Nadja smiled pleasantly.

"What was it like growing up in a carnival?"

"What do you mean?"

"I don't know — it just always seemed so glamorous to me. You know, being the visiting celebrities wherever you go."

"Well," Nadja noted dryly, "it's not quite like that. Mostly it's just a job. Sorry to disappoint you."

"I bet people come to you with some interesting problems." Ellie stuck her little finger into her champagne to stir and burst the bubbles, then sucked it clean. Nadja watched her for a moment, considering how truthful she dared be.

"There's only so many problems," she said, "and people just keep having them over and over. Lost rings, heart attacks, unplanned pregnancies, affairs, divorces. It's pretty boring after a while."

"Sounds just like Heaven," Ellie lamented, "only more so."

They drank for a while in silence, until the crickets felt safe and began to chirp. Ellie studied the cup in her hands, again overcome with shyness. "It sounds like we're way out in the country," she ventured, finally.

"They're in the heating vent," Nadja said. "If they bother you, throw a shoe at them and they'll shut up."

Ellie drained her cup. "How do you learn to tell fortunes?" she asked.

"Mostly just practice. It's like reading patterns and keeping an eye on the person. They kind of tell their own fortunes."

"Read my palm," Ellie said suddenly, and when she looked up into Nadja's eyes she felt a tremor of something alien and dangerous pass through her body.

Nadja reached for her hand, and Ellie blushed to realize how damp it was. She was sweating like the first time she held hands with Jack Wilson at the seventh-grade skating party.

"This is your life line, and this is your heart line, and this is your love line." Nadja traced the patterns with a light touch that thrilled Ellie. She hoped it wasn't obvious. "Now, if this represents your whole life, and this is where your love line crosses it, what do you guess that would mean?"

Ellie looked at the crosshatch of patterns on her palm. "That I'll fall in love when I'm forty-five?" asked Ellie, attempting levity.

"Actually, yes," said Nadja. "See? You don't even need me to tell you." She held Ellie's hand a moment longer, until neither of them could stand it, then released it and picked up her drink. "So I'm going to drive down to Ball Monday morning and put in an application to make canning jars."

"That's quite a ways to go to work."

"Well, they're not hiring at Hoosier Chemicals. You know of anything else around here?"

"Not since the bakery closed," admitted Ellie. And they settled back in their seats to drink and listen to the crickets. Each time they emptied their cups, Ellie poured more. It wasn't altogether too long till they'd finished the second bottle.

And it wasn't much more than a minute or two later that Ellie suddenly felt like flocks of birds were beating their wings on the inside of her stomach, trying to rise in flight. Oh god, she prayed, let me make it to the bathroom, let me not lose it, not just yet, and she lurched past Nadja down the hallway to the little bathroom where Charlene had been discovered. With not a second to spare. Nadja followed, standing just outside the room, and waited until the retching noises stopped to ask, "Are you okay?"

Ellie flushed the toilet. "Yeah," she called weakly. "I feel like a complete idiot, though."

"For getting drunk?"

"For throwing up."

"It's no big deal."

"I hate to throw up."

"It's all right."

"Champagne is a disgusting high, you know?" Ellie opened the bathroom door. Nadja nodded. "Why aren't you sick?"

"I am."

"You're not throwing up."

"I never throw up. I just feel like shit."

Ellie laughed, delighted at Nadja's blunt language. "That's too bad, really. It's sort of a relief to throw up."

"Believe me, I would if I could," Nadja assured her.

Ellie turned on the tap, scooped water into her hands and rinsed her mouth. "You can't throw up at all?" she asked when she finished.

"Huh-uh." Nadja shook her head. "Never could."

"I'm so drunk," Ellie observed, peering at her reflection in the mirror.

"I think you should stay here for the night," Nadja told her. "You aren't in any shape to go home."

"It's only five blocks," Ellie protested, but she was so pleased at Nadja's suggestion that she added quickly, "but you're right. I'd probably fall over halfway there. Then they'd take me to Fourth Floor County, with all the drunks from Pete's Gate."

"Could be fun," Nadja shrugged.

"Nah," said Ellie. "Drunks can't get it up." And she burst into laughter, amazed at her own daring. She had no idea whether Nadja would care for such ribald humor.

Nadja looked carefully at Ellie. "Are there any men in Heaven worth knowing?"

"Nah," said Ellie. "They're mostly married, and the ones that aren't are either weird or so awful their wives left 'em. And wives don't just leave husbands in Heaven, you know. So when they do, you know there's gotta be a good reason."

"So what do you do — you know — for 'companionship'?"

"Not much," said Ellie. "Personally," she added, "I prefer traveling salesmen. They move on out, they tell no tales, they don't expect you to wash their damn socks. 'Course you gotta listen to their stupid jokes."

"Isn't it kind of risky? I mean, you don't know who else they've slept with in their little voyages."

"They can't sell me nothin' if they don't use somethin'," Ellie said, slurring her words, and liking the way they sounded. "Actually, you know which one was the most fun?"

"Which one?"

"The guy who sold rubbers."

Nadja burst into laughter. "No kidding? Why? Did he have all those little French gizmos and stuff like that?"

"Yeah, but I never tried them. He was just a really funny guy. Fun to be with."

"So how do you meet a traveling rubber salesman in Heaven, Indiana?"

"Oh, they all show up at Clara's Kitchen. He came in one day and we got to talking. Said he was in the medical field. Preventative medicine. When I went back to the kitchen, Stell told me just exactly which diseases he was in the business of preventing.

"Well, the next day was my day off, so I met him at his next stop. It was great. And disease-free."

"What was he like?" Nadja asked. "I mean, besides being funny."

"He just had a sense of adventure." Ellie blushed. "I've never talked about this stuff before," she said. "I mean, who would I talk about it with?"

"Tell me about the first time you did it, "Nadja prompted. "How old were you?"

"Sixteen."

"Me, too."

"It was the summer my mom got sick. You know Seese at the beauty shop? Her husband Denny and his cousin, this guy named Archer, came into Clara's Kitchen one Saturday for lunch."

Nadja just nodded and listened. It was as if she had set up a magnetic field, and it was pulling the words right out of Ellie.

"So Denny introduces us, and then he says, 'Be nice to my cousin. He's here all the way from South Bend. Just broke up with his girlfriend, and he's shipping out to Nam tomorrow.' So then after they leave, I find a two-dollar tip. I mean, *no one* tips in Heaven, especially not anyone under twenty. So I'm thinking South Bend must be a pretty cosmopolitan place. Later in the afternoon, Arch comes back alone and asks me if I'd like to see a movie or something with him on his last night in the States. It was a choice between *Love Story* in Hartford City or *Airport* in Marion. I knew I didn't want to see *Love Story*. Seese had already told me about it — I think she saw it six times or something like that — and there were enough people dying at my house already that I didn't especially want to see it again on the screen, you know?"

Nadja nodded.

"So we went to *Airport*. Did you ever see it?"

Nadja shook her head no.

"Well, it was one of the first of those disaster-in-the-sky-type movies, only it was really slow. And I was only sort of half watching it, because Arch kept talking, making wisecracks. Jean Seberg was in it. Remember her?"

"*Joan of Arc?*"

"Yeah, that's the one. Arch made me laugh, talking about how they ought to light a fire under her, the way they did in *Joan of Arc*, to liven things up a little. I think that's the thing I like most in a guy. A sense of humor, you know?"

Nadja smiled.

"So anyway, then he starts whispering stuff in my ear. Like he hopes they put him on a plane for Nam that is as solid as the one in the movie, because the one in the movie is flying along with explosions and holes in it and all this stuff and it just keeps going. And it got to me, you know, that this guy was right there next to me, I mean his lips right there at my ear, and the next day he could be dead.

"So anyway, we went for fries and shakes afterwards, and he talked about how *Patton* was his favorite movie, and Patton was such an inspiration to him and all that. And then he drove me home, only he didn't go straight there, he went out by Hutter's Pond and we sat there for a while just looking at the water. And he's telling me how the girl he just broke up with didn't appreciate the sacrifice he was about to make for his country, and that he could tell I was a real patriot, and then he started to cry. But I mean, not really. Not like my dad used to cry when he was drunk on his butt, but kind of holding back, trying not to cry. So I'm blown away, you know? And he starts telling me all this stuff about how he wished he'd met me a year ago, and I'm the only one who has ever understood where he's really coming from, and I'm beautiful, and all this time he's got his hands down my blouse and up my skirt, and, well, next thing I know, he's putting it in me. I had no idea it would hurt so much. Did you? Know it would hurt the first time?"

Nadja shook her head. "Huh-uh," she said.

"So then he drove me home, and that was that. I remember looking in the mirror and wondering if other people could tell."

Nadja smiled and nodded. "Did he come back all right from Vietnam?" she asked.

"He never went. I ran into Seese a couple of weeks later and asked how he was doing, and she tells me about how he's really bad news, that he got his girlfriend pregnant and then ditched her and had flunked out of Notre Dame and was going down south to some college that was basically for guys who were dodging the draft by being in the Reserves."

"Hmmm."

"But you know, even though he was a jerk, I kind of didn't mind. I mean..." She blushed again. "I might still be an old maid, if it wasn't for Arch."

"Weren't there any other guys around?"

"Yeah, but they were local. They always talked too much."

"So that's why the salesmen."

"Uh-huh. But not just any salesman. Not the depressing ones. The best ones aren't really salesmen. Like the guy who sold plant soil. He was really in training as a manager, and was only out on the route to learn the routine so he could be a better supervisor."

"What happened to him?"

"I don't know. He had a wife and a couple of kids, and they were about to move to Pennsylvania. I mean, that's kind of what I liked about him. He wasn't dead-end. He was on his way to Somewhere Else. Okay," Ellie said. "Now it's your turn. How did you lose your virginity?"

"The manager of Midways Unlimited," Nadja said. "But it wasn't really because I wanted to."

"Have you ever been in love?"

"I thought I was for a while. I dated the Thinnest Man in the World for six years."

"No kidding?"

"No kidding. But then he took off with a fan dancer, and it turned out I didn't even miss him, so I guess that's not really what you'd call love."

"How was it, you know, doing it with the Thinnest Man in the World? What was he like in bed?"

"All skin and *bone*," Nadja said, and they both collapsed in a fit of schoolgirl giggles.

"Here's to sex," said Ellie, lifting her empty glass in the air.

"Here's to rubbers," said Nadja, clinking her glass to Ellie's.

"And here's to old friends."

"To old friends."

"And to getting drunk once in a while."

"To getting drunk. Once in a while."

"And here's to sleep." Ellie put her glass down. "I'm about to fall over."

"Wait a minute." Nadja jumped up, went into the kitchen, and came back with a glass of water and some tablets.

"What's this?"

"Vitamins. Take them now, and you won't have so much of a hangover in the morning."

Ellie swallowed the pills and sank back into the couch, then leaned to the side and let herself fall over. Nadja brought a blanket and bed pillow, tucked her in, and said good night. Ellie fell asleep with a smile on her face.

When she woke the next day, Ellie noticed that the sky was unusually blue. It was almost as if her vision had cleared, now that all those never-said words weren't plugging up her brain anymore.

Stella and Lester noticed it, too. One morning while Ellie wiped down the tables, Stella leaned over to Lester as she filled his cup. "It does a person good to have a friend," she said. "That's the most energy I've seen in that girl since the day I met her."

"It brings out her natural beauty," Lester agreed, then realized the potential inappropriateness of his remark and added "doncha think?" to make it Stella's observation rather than his own.

"Yes, it does," Stella nodded.

Then Granny and Wilma Porter came in for coffee and Stella went over to sit with them a spell, and take a load off her feet.

· ·

LESTER DIDN'T KNOW QUITE WHAT POSSESSED HIM to invite Ellie to go to the fair with him. He hadn't prowled the midways since that unfortunate scene in the truck, out behind the livestock exhibits. But he still loved carnivals, fairs, even circuses, and more or less on an impulse that September morning he asked Ellie if she'd like to go along for the day. Ellie agreed almost at once. She hadn't been to a fair since the fall of her junior year in high school. That was with Jerry Burney. It had been first a tedious, then an annoying, and finally a terrifying trip as Jerry went from simply self-centered to slightly drunk and finally totally plastered on the fifth of Johnny Walker he'd stored in his jacket pocket and insisted on sampling while they drove. By the time they got to the Howard County Fairgrounds, Ellie was embarrassed to be with him and afraid to make him take her home. When he got bored and wanted to leave, she whined and wheedled to stay a little longer, and a little longer still, till she thought he might be sober enough to drive and she'd have a passing chance of getting home alive. So now Ellie asked Lester just one question before she agreed to accompany him. "Are you one of these fellows that gets so tanked up he can't drive home straight?"

"Naw," Lester laughed. "Black coffee's my drink."

They went on the last day. The weather promised to be perfect: warm and sunny, but with enough breeze to keep the air fresh.

Lester's first requirement was to look at the prize pigs. Then he had to check the cows and chickens. He also looked at championship corn, while Ellie marveled at quilts and wondered if she could ever accomplish something like that: so beautiful and so practical at the same time. Except who would want to put something that beautiful to practical use?

The carnival midway was the next attraction. They actually entered it from the rear, past the tent proclaiming "Girls, Girls, Girls!" They toured the Ten-in-One, featuring the Wild Snake Woman of the West; the Amazing Human Skeleton; the Tattooed Man, who could make the naked girl on his biceps sway her hips and nod her head; the Fabulous Fortune-Telling Fatt Family; the Human Calculating Calendar; Torcha the Fire-Eating Queen; two pairs of Siamese twins, who sang barbershop quartets together; a contortionist known as the Pretzel Girl; Jack and the Giant (a man three feet tall and his eight-foot partner, who did a tumbling act together); and the Tiger Woman, whose act consisted of riding once around the tent pit on her tiger's back, then ceremoniously putting plugs in her ears and placing her head in the tiger's mouth while it roared. Lester told Ellie about his days in India during World War II, where he saw pinheads and midgets, and a baby with two extra feet growing out of its stomach. "They had a lot of pinheads over there," said Lester, "and just plain deformed people. I always figured, hell, at least they got a way to make a living. The poor bastards that were normal just starved. Nothing to make people want to look at them. But they probably all woulda done a damn sight better if they just had some plain medical attention. They used to have pinheads in the carnivals here, too. But nowadays you don't see the kind of freaks you used to see. People got all up in arms about the exploitation. That's why each of these have some kind of act they do. Even the Fatts have their little mind-reading gimmick. They can't just set there weighing a ton anymore. But they're pretty good, ain't they? Especially that Lenore. How'd you suppose she knew about that lady's arthritis?"

In the middle of the midway were the rides: twenty-three in all. Lester suggested the Ferris wheel, and Ellie reluctantly agreed. She was afraid she'd be afraid. But Lester promised to set a good example for her by remaining calm. Ellie felt ridiculous. At thirty-two, she felt more like an awkward teenager than a grown woman. And with Lester she felt an odd confusion, like she couldn't tell if he was her grandfather or her date.

They got into the last car, so Ellie had no period of adjustment, no slow ascent to the top while she got her composure worked out. The thing just took off, and Ellie gasped a little bit and grabbed at Lester's hand. He had to laugh. Something about her was so — well — he didn't exactly know the word for it. As much as he talked, words weren't really his specialty. But there was something about her that made him feel the way he did the first time he flew in an airplane. Amazed, kind of. He reached around her shoulder and squeezed it reassuringly. "First Ferris wheel was two hundred and some feet high," he said. "This is just a little guy."

Ellie looked ill. "You want off?" Lester asked. "We can tell him to stop and let us off."

Ellie shook her head. "I'm going to enjoy this," she said grimly. Then: "You know what I want when I get off this alive? A sno-kone." And she turned to the task of relaxing, which she accomplished by saying silently to herself, "It's almost over. It's almost over. It's almost over."

When they got off the ride, Lester held his hand out to help Ellie down from the cab, and she didn't let it go right away. There was something strange happening to her body, and she felt a little jelly-kneed. Lester led her down the midway past the shooting galleries, the coin tosses, and the popcorn and cotton-candy stands.

Ellie followed, absorbed in the sensations that made her feel giddy and off-balance.

Near the front of the midway they stopped by the sno-kone cart. "What flavor?" asked Lester. "My treat."

Ellie looked over the choices. The colors all looked poison-
ous. "Were they always this gross looking?" she asked.

"I expect so," said Lester. "How 'bout a lemonade instead?"
He gestured across the midway to the stand.

The cold lemonade kind of settled Ellie into herself again.
And she noted that just beyond the lemonade stand, imme-
diately inside the gateway to the carnival, stood the fortune-
teller's tent.

"D'ya ever get your fortune told, Lester?" Ellie wanted
to know.

"Oh, once," Lester allowed. "Once I went in with Helen."

"What did you find out?"

"Nothing I didn't already know."

"You know, Nadja used to be a fortune-teller. Don't tell
anyone, now. She made me promise not to tell anyone. She
used to read people's plates. Like some of them read tea leaves
when you're finished with your tea. She'd read what people
leave on their plates."

"That a fact?"

"Yeah. You should get her to read your plate sometime at
Clara's. Except then she'd know I told you."

"Why'd she give it up?"

"She said too many people took her seriously. It made her
nervous. And I guess she got tired of traveling around all the
time. She's not really a Gypsy, you know, but they always said
she was, in the carnivals. She and her granny. Her granny had
a little joke. She called herself some Gypsy word that meant
"not a Gypsy," and people thought it was a real Gypsy name.
Her real name is Nancy White."

"Is that a fact?" Lester looked at Ellie sucking lemonade
through her straw and thought to himself, *I'm old enough to
be her grandfather.*

"That's a fact," Ellie said, and thought to herself, *he really
does look a little like Cary Grant.* It occurred to her that he
would have as much at stake as she would in maintaining a

good reputation in Heaven, so perhaps he could be trusted with the secret of the mysterious little stairway that ran from the back of Clara's Kitchen directly to her basement. This was something she hadn't even told Nadja about, and she'd told Nadja about as much as she'd told everyone else in her life all wrapped up together.

"Lester?"

"Yes, ma'am?"

"Can you keep a secret?"

Lester saw a look on her face that prompted him to ask an equally important question. "I can," he assured her. "Can you?"

. . .

"I get too rooted," Ellie was saying, "not like I want to be. I want to go careening through the air like a dandelion seed that someone blew on a balmy kind of day. The kind that wafts up and picks up an air current way above the trees even, goes to the next county, catches another breeze, sails on over a state line or two, looks down on the little cars on the little roads driving past the little houses with the people too little to even see. Just wafts and wafts, floats and dips, and surges at times, then drifts, then swoops up again and off, maybe even over an ocean, finds at last but only at long last an interesting nook, a bit of hospitable soil to settle in. Then and only then sends a tentative root down to feel out the possibilities. But I'm lacking the right fluff, I guess. Not enough fluff to overcome this Midwest humidity. It weighs me down, forces a landing on me, crashes me down in my own backyard where the clay takes root in me, holds me to the Indiana earth. I feel heavy, rooted like the dandelion that you can never dig out because there's always a piece of it that breaks off and sticks.

"Now Nadja — she's like a soaring kind of seed. She could zip up there blown by a lover, settle on a passing bird and ride her way to the South Pole, or maybe Africa, or Tierra del Fuego or the Canary Islands. I think from moving around all the time, she knows how to move. I just come from a family of stubborn weed roots, is all. I'm gonna have to rip myself up to ever get out of here."

Ellie turned onto her side to look for Lester's reaction. That's when she noticed he was asleep.

She smiled a sigh, turned out the little lamp on the nightstand, and rolled against him. His steady breath soothed her, till she too slept.

· ·

NADJA WORKED AT THE GLASS FACTORY NOW, running equipment that churned out row upon row of canning jars. Granny had taken to frequenting Clara's Kitchen at lunchtime. She and Stella got along in some kind of way that sort of surprised everybody. For one thing, Granny was a good listener, and Stella loved to talk. For another thing, one of Stella's uncles had been in the carny business, a ballyhooer. So Stella had spent a lot of her younger summers at the Great Hoosier Expo shows, and she even remembered some of the folks Granny knew. Granny had worked for a lot of different shows, and she knew a lot of people. She'd never met Stella's uncle, but she sure knew the outfit he'd worked for just before he died. She remembered hearing about his death, too, some six years before. Stella's uncle Theo had been helping to strike the front of the show when his heart gave out.

At seventy-eight, he'd been in the business for sixty-four years, and there must have been three, four hundred people at his funeral. He was buried on a Monday, so folks could get there and still be on to their next stop by Wednesday. They held the funeral down in Richmond, and Stella made the trip. Theo had lived in Richmond all his life, was born in one of those houses that blew up in the big explosion they had there back in…'65, was it? Quite a funeral, with all the ten-in-one performers Theo had introduced over the years. One of the sword-swallowers delivered the eulogy. Said Theo was no doubt turning the tip to see the angels now. Stella hadn't been sure that was really such a respectful thing to say, but she'd had to smile even so. Uncle Theo would have liked it.

Stella especially enjoyed Granny's company because Walter was retreating further and further into his own world these days, and Granny always listened sympathetically when Stella told of Walter's latest tricks, like putting the telephone in the toilet, or wearing his terry-cloth bathrobe on his legs like some kind of Siamese pajamas. Stella kept him with her now at the restaurant because she couldn't trust him on his own.

Granny gave Walter some tea that helped clear his mind some, and Stella was so impressed she added it to the menu. She called it Wake-Up Tea.

She served it the day they celebrated Clara's 100th birthday. This was the Clara, of course, for whom Clara's Kitchen was named. Hers was the recipe for Dutch Oven Chicken that everybody agreed couldn't be beat, and for the thin egg noodles that went into Sunday's soup. Clara had retired thirty-two years before, when Stella bought the place. For the past twenty years, since Chester died, she'd lived over at Westwind Nursing Home.

Her son James, who was himself now retired (from lawyering) came back from his home in Florida to take part in the affair. He'd been president of the senior class in 1933, when Lester entered his freshman year. In fact, he'd dated Helen a time or two back then. But he'd gone off to DePauw, and married a girl from out of state. She came from quite a bit of money, and they originally settled down near her folks, in the Baltimore area.

The wife couldn't come to Clara's birthday party because she'd broken her hip and couldn't travel for at least six weeks. She and James had two daughters and a son who did manage to come to Heaven for their grandmother's big celebration. Then altogether seven great-grandchildren showed up, and one great-great-granddaughter. Named Clara after the guest of honor, she was three months old and teething. Granny had a special tea for her, too.

It was during this party that it came to light that Nadja could read plates. The daughter of Stella's uncle Theo, who went to college at Ball State with Clara's daughter Rose — the one who died back in '50 of polio — came to the party. And she got to talking with Granny. And it turned out she remembered Granny from back when she was with Midwest Midways, and she remembered Nadja too, of course. Now, Nadja was there helping Ellie wait tables for the party, and couldn't deny that she was the one who read the plates.

So Uncle Theo's daughter, Celena was her name, brought Nadja out of retirement. And by the time the party was over and Charles was delivering a tired and bewildered Clara back to Westwind, Nadja had read the crumbs of chocolate cake and ice cream for over two dozen people, beginning with Clara and including most of the out-of-town guests. When she saw Wendell's tumor that had just been diagnosed the week before by a doctor in Fort Wayne that no one knew about but Wendell, folks got really interested. When she told Saralynn Peterson that she was pregnant again, Saralynn gasped because it was true, but she hadn't told a soul — except her husband Jack, of course, who swore he hadn't told a soul either. Then when she saw Mae's first husband's heart attack when everyone knew that had happened years before Nadja ever heard of Heaven, and saw how it was still affecting Mae's life, which everyone except Mae could see clear as day, they knew she had a gift. She finally had to promise that she'd come back to Clara's Kitchen Friday after work and read the folks' supper plates that she hadn't had time to do at the party. Stella spoke up at that point, and commented that it didn't seem fair to ask her to do all this for free. How about a Fortune-Teller Special, she asked the folks. "I'll make up a dinner with beets, roast beef, mashed potatoes and gravy. You can get the dinner for the usual special price, and have Nadja read the plate when you're done, for an extra five dollars." Everyone agreed that seemed like a more than reasonable price. Nadja didn't have much to say in the matter. She just kind of sat there taking it all in and paying close attention to everybody there without seeming to pay attention at all. Granny just sat there too, nodding slightly in approval and pride.

Clara's Kitchen had always been a popular place in town. It helped that it was the only restaurant, except for the Happy Burger over by the shopping plaza, and folks were naturally loyal to it. But when the Friday Night Fortune-Teller Special went into effect, business took off through the roof. Pretty soon they had to make it the Weekend Fortune-Teller Special, which meant Friday and Saturday, because Stella knew better than to have anything that smacked of the occult in the place on Sunday. There was an element, she knew, that would for certain get up in arms about that. They had almost picketed her back when she made the decision to be open on Sundays at all, but she had neatly sidestepped them by advertising in *Heaven's Sentinel*, the weekly newspaper, that she was going to stay open on Sundays in order to encourage people to go to church. If they didn't have to worry about cooking Sunday dinner, she reasoned, they'd have more time to devote to Christian worship on the Lord's Day. That kind of took the wind out of the sails of the folks who were against any doing business on Sunday, but it didn't by a long shot mean they weren't waiting for a chance to bring the subject up again, given half a chance. Stella knew to stick with just Friday and Saturday for something as controversial as fortune-telling.

Now you'd think a thing like that would die down after a few weeks. After all, there weren't all that many new customers, and pretty soon the regulars had all had a chance to have their plates read. But Nadja was good at it, and a lot of people just wanted to come back a second or third or fourth time to get an update. Then too, the word began to leak out to the other towns nearby, and people who didn't ordinarily come to Heaven started making the trip.

One Saturday night after she closed the place, Stella called Nadja into the kitchen. She showed her the bottom of the gravy pot. Stella had forgotten to turn the heat off, and the little bit of gravy left in the bottom had scorched and cracked. Just for fun, she wanted Nadja to see if it had anything to tell her.

"Well," said Nadja, "first thing to know is that since it's not your plate, it's not your fortune."

"Whose would it be, then?"

"I'm not sure. Maybe a little of everyone's who ate the gravy. Maybe you, if you made it."

"I started it," Stella said, "Ellie stirred it, I caught Walter eating it from the pot, and then I forgot about it and burnt it."

"So it could be just about anybody's fortune," said Nadja. "I'll see what I can see."

She couldn't have looked at it for more than about five seconds before she glanced back up at Stella and told her they'd better check on Walter before they went any further. Sure enough, he was out in front getting into trouble. He had dumped an entire bottle of ketchup all over the top of the counter and was rubbing it carefully onto every inch of the surface.

"What are you up to, Walter." Stella's voice was tired but remarkably patient.

"Oh, I just thought I'd help you clean up," Walter replied mildly.

Stella winked at Nadja, and moved to distract Walter with another cup of tea. Nadja brought the pot out where she could read it while Stella cleaned the ketchup and kept an eye on her addled husband. Nadja peered again into the blackened depths of the pot. Stella caught her puzzled expression.

"So what do you see?"

"Where's the secret passageway?"

Stella pretended ignorance. "The what?"

"I'm seeing some sort of secret passageway," Nadja persisted. "Someone's hiding in it."

"Someone used to hide in it," Stella corrected, an implicit admission that she'd understood the first time. "It was an underground railroad station. So how do you do this? Is it really a psychic gift?"

"Nothing," said Nadja, "is exactly as it seems. Does it seem like a psychic gift?"

"It sure does," said Stella.

Nadja just smiled.

"Well." Stella finished sponging the last bit of ketchup. "I guess I'd better scrub that pot."

"Just soak it," Nadja counseled. "Stick in a little soap and water, and wood ashes if you've got any. Let time loosen it up for you."

"You don't say?" Stella raised her eyebrows in mild surprise. "Wood ashes? Like from the barbecue pit?"

"Uh-huh," Nadja confirmed.

"So what does it mean, this secret passageway?"

"I don't know," Nadja admitted. "I guess my powers are all used up for the night."

On the way home, Nadja walked by Ellie's house. She thought about stopping in to say hello, but decided against it. It was, after all, well past nine, and the only light seemed to be coming from the basement. She's evidently got company already, thought Nadja.

Down in her basement, Ellie pushed the massive shelves back into place. Then she took Lester by the hand and led him up to her bed.

And at Clara's Kitchen, Stella sat Walter down by the door in the storeroom while she contemplated whether to ask Ellie when she'd discovered the passageway, and what use she'd put it to. She decided against it. Stella's mother had always said, "What you don't know can't hurt you." Stella thought that was a pretty reasonable philosophy of life. She didn't go looking for trouble, and it generally left her alone.

• • •

Seese got Helen settled in the chair, ready for a shampoo, then buzzed over to check on Minnie. "Scalp doing okay?"

She touched the curlers lightly, so the tightly wound hair would not be pulled or loosened.

"Oh, I'm fine. You go ahead and get Helen taken care of." She picked up a *Ladies' Home Journal* and began to thumb through it.

"How about this Indian summer?" Seese asked whoever cared to listen, as she wet down Helen's hair.

"Oh, my, yes," Minnie responded instantly.

"They say it'll cool off by Wednesday," Helen added. "You know nothing good ever lasts."

"So what's this I hear about Wasmuth's Funeral Home going out of business?" Seese actually knew the answer to her own question, but she also knew it pleased Minnie to be the first to know things. Her success as a hairdresser was due only in part to her skills with comb and scissors. The rest were what you'd call her people skills. Seese had plenty of people skills.

"Why, they say there just aren't enough people dying any-more to make it worthwhile," Minnie answered. Helen, head covered in suds, just snorted. Minnie continued, "You know, there's just so many folks leaving the area. Of course, the young ones always did tend to leave, going off to college or the cities or whatnot. But now it's the ones retiring. They head up to Minnesota or down to Florida. Herb Wasmuth says if he could afford it, he'd move down there too. Says he bets you could do real well in the funeral business down there."

"I don't know what people think they'll find when they go," Helen said, as Seese sat her up and rubbed a thick towel through her hair. "If you ask me, a person would do well to stay right here in Heaven. It's as close as some folks will ever get!"

Seese laughed. "Are you saying we're a town of sinners?"

Minnie opined, "Nobody's perfect."

"No," Helen agreed. "Nobody's perfect. Everybody makes mistakes." Then she astonished Seese, Minnie, and herself by announcing, "I want my hair cut short today."

"Are you sure? I wouldn't want you coming in tomorrow saying, 'Put it back.' Why, you've never had more than a trim in all the years you've been coming in here. You have such beautiful long hair — even when it's up on your head. Are you sure you want to cut it all off?"

"I'm tired of it and I want it off," Helen said, a little impatiently. "Cut it short, and curl it, too. And dye it black. Like Minnie's."

Minnie flushed with pleasure.

Seese took a breath. "Okay," she said, "Last chance to back out." Then she began to cut. Helen's long, thick hair fell to the floor, a grey nest at the base of the chair. "Does Lester know you're doing this?"

"I don't suppose he does."

"Well, he's in for a surprise."

"Yes, I guess he is."

"You're my witness, Minnie. You heard her tell me to do this."

"Yes, I surely did."

"You know what?" Seese said. "I think this is going to look terrific. You won't even need that much of a perm. With all that weight off, your hair is naturally curly. Did you know that?"

"What?"

"That you have naturally curly hair? Was it always like this?"

"Always," Helen said.

• • •

What with Lester a regular on weekday mornings and Nadja coming in on weekend evenings, it took a while for him to get around to coming in to get his plate read. "You oughta bring Helen down here, Les," Stella told him. "Didn't she used to like going to fortune-tellers?" So Lester finally got around to it one Saturday night. He didn't really tell Helen the plan at first, because he wasn't sure she'd want to see a fortune-teller again. But if this little gal was as good as everyone said she was, why, maybe she could tell them something useful.

113

Truth was, now that he was getting on in years, he too found himself thinking somewhat obsessively about what ever happened to the baby girl he'd delivered out in the barn that August night back during the Centennial. He tried a time or two to bring up the question with his wife, but she persisted in adhering to her official version of the story, even with him.

"Mother," Lester would say, because he had always called her Mother, even before Melinda was born, except for the dozen years that he was Harley and she was Missus Breck, "Where did you take that little baby?"

"What little baby are you talking about," she'd say.

"Why, Melinda's little baby, of course," Lester would respond, whereupon Helen would look at him as if he were the one who had gone crazy, and say, "Why, Lester Breck, you know very well I don't have any idea where she left that baby."

So Lester had long since given up on getting anything out of Helen.

This Saturday night he told her he wanted to take her shopping over at Hutter Plaza to get a few things for the house. Helen protested that she didn't need anything new for the house. "Well," said Lester, "Why don't you come along while I do my shopping, then, and keep me company."

Helen was frankly pleased. She hadn't told a soul, but the fact was that Helen knew Lester was carrying on again. She couldn't prove anything, but she just kind of had an instinct for when Lester was lying. So when he came home a time or three at seven in the morning and told her he'd been staying with his sick friend Maurice, she figured something was up. This time, however, she didn't banish him to the barn. He was too old for that. And truth be known, Helen liked having him in the house. She determined to win him back, fair and square. Other than to church and her monthly visit to Seese's, Lester had not voluntarily taken her anyplace in years. But now he was asking for her company! Maybe it was the new hairdo.

"I got to get dinner on," Helen protested.

"Why don't you take a break from cooking tonight. We'll get supper at Stella's," Lester suggested. "She's got a good beef and gravy special on Friday, Saturday nights."

Helen shot a piercing look at Lester. "You want to ask that Gypsy woman something?"

"Oh, you heard about her?" Lester kept his voice casual, offhand.

"'Course I heard about her. You don't have something like that come into town without everybody knowing about it," Helen snorted.

"They say she's pretty good," Lester allowed.

"Why don't you go on down to do your shopping, and I'll think about going to Stella's for dinner," Helen said. "You know I hate to shop. But if you want to see that Gypsy woman, I'll go with you. I have to tell you, though, I don't expect anything. They're all a bunch of liars and thieves."

When Lester got back from the hardware store, Helen was waiting for him. She was dressed in her best church dress and was pacing back and forth in the kitchen. "Get some decent clothes on," she urged. "And don't take all night doing it. I told Stell we'd be there by six. You never used to have to make a reservation."

At Clara's Kitchen, Lester ate his food steadily, as always. And as always, he began by shaking salt and pepper over everything on the plate, then mixing it all together with his knife and fork. The brown beef gravy mingled with blood-red beet juice and mashed potatoes to form a thick reddish-brown soup that Lester used as a sauce on the meat and beets. Helen's approach was meticulous, the opposite of Lester's. She ate a bite from the meat, then one from the potatoes, then one from the beets. Her bites were carefully measured to insure that the diminishing amounts of food items stayed in proportion to each other. She continued until there was one bit of each left on the plate. These she left. Helen usually ate everything on her plate, a habit no doubt left from Depression days, when plates were never full enough nor frequently enough served.

"Aren't you going to finish?" Lester asked.

"I want her to have something to read." Helen was impatient. "How's she going to read a mess like that?" And Helen nodded toward the brown-red stains on Lester's plate. Lester let the subject drop.

Stella appeared at the table with a full coffeepot, and poured refills. "You want to get your plates read tonight?"

"Well, Mother, what do you say?" Lester smiled at Helen. "Should we do it?"

"Of course," Helen said bluntly. "It's why you brought me here."

Stella winked at Lester with an implicit promise to send Nadja right over, and disappeared again.

For these occasions, Nadja wore a subdued version of her carnival outfit. A colorful scarf held her hair down and back. She wore a blouse with billowing sleeves, and a long flowery skirt that reached her ankles. Several thin silver bracelets dangled on each wrist, and rings circled the fourth and fifth fingers of each hand.

Lester and Helen watched her walk to their table. "Good evening," Nadja said, then stood waiting for an invitation to join them. "Stella said you would like me to read your plates? Who would like to be first?"

"Read them together," Helen commanded.

"All right," Nadja said, pulling up a chair between them. "I can do that. Do you have a particular question, or would you like me to just tell you what I see in general?"

"Find our grandchild." Helen was not one for beating around the bush.

Nadja looked at the smears on Lester's plate and the three neatly saved bites on Helen's. "Your grandchild is about my age?" she asked. "Thirty-five, thirty-six?"

"She...or he...would be that, yes." Lester had done a quick calculation in his head. Helen had no need to calculate. She had always known precisely how old the grandchild would be at any given time since the day she abandoned it.

"And this is your only child's child," Nadja continued. Both nodded. "And the mother...did she die?" Nadja asked hesitantly, carefully. Lester started to answer, but Helen cut him off. "Childbirth fever, they said."

Nadja looked at her. "And you have never seen the child?"

Intent now on the reading, Lester and Helen stared at the plates, wondering what revelation was written on them. They shook their heads no. Nadja smiled a small, sad, private smile. "So the child was left somewhere? Perhaps found by a kind stranger? That's what happened to me."

"We don't know," Lester said.

"Maybe there never was a child." Helen shot a piercing look at Nadja.

"See this?" Nadja pointed to a thin line of beet juice on Helen's plate running to the bit of mashed potatoes, then lifted her eyes to return Helen's gaze. "It's a cord. The child is alive. It is still connected to you. There are times when it has been quite close to you, others when it has been far away."

"Will we ever find her?" Lester broke the small silence that hung in the air after Nadja's last remark. If either of the others noticed his choice of pronoun, they didn't mention it.

"There are three secrets in the way," she said finally. "I can't be sure. But see here — " she pointed to Lester's plate, to a small stream of intermingled gravy and beet juice that ran by a lump of beet-stained potatoes. "See how this is a river, and it runs into an obstacle here, but it finds its way around? The situation is not impossible. I can tell you that much for sure."

Helen looked contemptuously at Nadja. "Let's go, Lester. She doesn't know any more than the rest of them."

She stood and pushed her chair back. "I'll be in the car," she announced, and strode out. Lester shrugged apologetically. "She's had a hard time with this," he said. He placed twelve dollars on the table, and handed Nadja a ten.

"I don't want it," Nadja said, and for a moment there was a shock in the air between them.

Lester swallowed to stifle the unexpected sob that rose to his throat. "I didn't really expect this to lead to anything," he admitted. "Still, a body always hopes."

Nadja looked into the old man's eyes. *You are my name*, she thought. *I am your grief.* "It's a girl. I know," she said aloud. "And she's alive. I know that, too. And she's not all that far from you."

"I'll tell Helen," Lester sighed. "Thank you, miss." And turning abruptly to avoid crying in public, he followed the path Helen had taken out to the parking lot.

"G'night, Les," Stella called. "See you Monday?"

"Yep," Lester called back. "G'night."

Stella came over to the table then, where Nadja still sat staring after them. "It's such a sad story," she said. "Like I was telling your granny the other day, Heaven has sure seen its share of heartbreak. You'd think with a name like that, it'd be easier for folks."

. . .

One morning in the dead of winter when the glass factory was closed for inventory, Nadja came in to have breakfast. Lester was there, as usual. Ellie was on her break, sitting with Lester, so she motioned Nadja over to join them. It was funny that in a town as small as Heaven, the two parts of her life were so separate. Lester, whom she saw almost every morning at Clara's, was rarely around when she saw Nadja, in the early evening hours after they both got off work. She'd talked to each about the other, and had even finally confessed the secret of the passageway and clandestine affair to Nadja. But the only time Nadja and Lester had actually come face to face before was on the night he'd brought Helen down to get their plates read.

"I don't know if there's going to be enough work at the factory," Nadja was saying.

"Yep," agreed Lester. "Maurice was telling me that they're talking about a layoff. His nephew works down there in R & D.

118

He says they just can't compete, with all that old equipment. Same thing that happened back in '72 at the bakery."

"And I heard they're about to lay off at the chemical plant, too," Ellie added.

"Like they say," Stella chimed in from behind the counter, "business in Heaven is going You Know Where!"

"How did this place get its name, anyway?" Nadja wanted to know.

"Les, tell her that story they wrote up back during the Centennial," Stella said, then interrupted him before he could start. "Seems it was named by coloreds, come up escaping slavery." Stella crossed the room to sit with the small group.

Lester took over. "Well, they called it Rockville in those days, because it seemed like the only place in Indiana where there were more rocks than trees. But you see, our founding father John Hutter was an abolitionist."

"When he built the first house here, he built it to be part of the Underground Railroad," Stella explained.

"I thought you wanted me to tell the story," Lester protested, feigning irritation.

"Go ahead and tell it. I'm not stopping you, I'm just helping out once in a while." Stella wiped a small spot of coffee from the table next to Lester's cup. Lester grinned at Nadja and continued.

"As I was saying, Hutter was in that there antislavery society. So quite a few slaves come up through here on their way further north. Now this one couple, Philip and Mary their names were, got here just about in time for Mary to give birth. She had a little boy named Peter. But she had a hard time with the birthing, and had to stay put and get her health back for quite a while. Wellsir, during that time I guess John Hutter just took a liking to them, so he went down to Kentucky and bought their freedom for them.

" 'Course, as it turned out, that didn't necessarily help once they come up with the Compromise of 1850."

"What was that?" Nadja asked.

Stella helped out again. "It was an agreement between the North and the South. It gave slaveholders the right to come up north and recapture runaways."

"So one day," Lester continued, "the county marshall comes ridin' up with three big fellas and says Philip and Mary gotta go back. Imagine that. Here they'd been livin' free almost a year. And by that time Mary was wet-nursing one of the Hutter babies, 'cause Mrs. Hutter — that's the great-great-grand-mother of Hutter's Dry Goods — had died in childbirth. And so she could take care of the Hutter baby, she had her own little boy sucking on what they called a sugar tit, back in the cabin she and Philip had built. Wellsir, those fellows come ridin' up and the first thing they did was go right to the Hutters'. Guess everybody knew she'd be there. And tried to grab her right away from that little Hutter baby. She hung on tight and the baby hung on tight to her, and one of those fellows just whipped out a knife like he was going to just cut the baby away from her.

"Now I guess that must've snapped that marshall to his senses about the kind of people he was dealing with. Not that he cottoned to colored folks. Never did, according to that Centennial newspaper story. But he was a decent man and a Christian, and that was just too much for him, I guess. 'Now you just wait a minute,' he says, 'as far as we know, these here folks have their Free Papers.' And he tells Mary to go get the papers to show the bounty hunters.

"Well, she heads out to the cabin to get those papers, but there's another one of them bounty hunters there, and the old-est Hutter girl is holding Peter and saying no they can't take that baby because it belongs to her. He was a pretty light-skinned baby, I guess. And she yells to Mary to run and don't come back. Mary knows the tunnels, of course, and she's gone.

They take Philip away, even with his Free Papers. The marshall says they'll have to show them to the judge, and that's the end of Philip."

"Aren't you forgetting something, Les?" Stella teased.

"What's that?" Lester asked.

"I think you were going to tell Nadja how the town got named," she reminded him.

"Didn't I say that?"

"No, you didn't."

"Well, they say it was when Philip and Mary first got here. They said it was like being in Heaven to be able to walk around free. So when the town incorporated that year, they decided Heaven was a prettier name than Rockville."

"They never found out what happened to Mary?" Ellie asked.

"Some say she got caught out past Pleasant Ridge, trying to get to Ohio. Others say she kept going, made it all the way up to Canada."

"And just left her baby behind?"

"Well, there's one version of the story says she tried to come back and was caught, another says she lived wild in the woods but always looked after him from a distance. Then some say she even come back, years later when she was an old woman, to try to find him. But by then, you see, he was gone. Those that hold to that version say she went and threw herself in the bog. They say her bones are down there still. But that's just a story they tell the kids at Halloween. Fact of the matter is, no one knows.

"But that little baby Peter grew up and doncha know married the Hutter girl that his mother had been wet-nursing the day she ran off. Looked more like an Indian than a colored. And they had a couple of kids, I guess.

"Then after the Reconstruction — well, by that time the town had grown a lot, lotta new folks not like the Hutters. Lotta folks up from the South. They passed a sundown law. Then somehow one of 'em found out the story of Philip, and they got up a nighttime visit, with their sheets on and all, ran Peter and Betsy out of town. They moved on up to Fort Wayne, I believe the story went. One of their grandchildren used to come through here every once in a while in the forties. Was a traveling preacher. Don't know what ever happened to him.

"Well, anyway, that's how Heaven got its name, as far as I know."

"So there's no descendants of them here?" Ellie was fascinated.

"Not that anyone knows of. It's been an all-white town as long as I can remember," Lester said.

Nadja was silent.

Stella poured more coffee.

THE YEARS PASS SUBTLY IN A PLACE LIKE HEAVEN. Not much changes. Folks grow older, and every so often someone dies. Not too many babies are born these days, because so many of the young people move to bigger towns and cities. They get jobs at Wal-Mart or Eli Lilly or go off to college and never come back. At holiday times the town grows. It's a place people like to come back to, as long as they don't have to stay.

At Thanksgiving, they pack the kids in the car and drive across Route 40 or down 31 and turn onto the smaller state roads that eventually will lead them to the sign that says "Welcome to Heaven." There's one of these signs at each end of Main Street right at the town limits, and one at each end of First. You can't get into Heaven without being welcomed to it.

Some of the parents will be singing "Over the river and through the woods" as they drive. It will make them feel that they are passing on valuable traditions to their children.

The old folks stand at their windows and either thank God for keeping the weather clear, or implore Him to get their children and grandchildren and occasionally even great-grand-children safely through the falling snow.

Those in the middle generation deliberately estimate their arrival time to be two hours later than they reasonably believe it will be, to minimize the worrying they know their parents will do. When they arrive, everyone exclaims about being early and making good time. If they do run into delays on the way, you can bet they'll call before the anticipated hour. It's a town where people go out of their way to worry, and go out of their way not to cause worry.

At Christmas, even more families come back. This time the ones who've gone east or west to a coast, or south to warmer climates, fly in to Indianapolis or Fort Wayne or Kokomo and rent a car to drive up or down or over.

It's a Norman Rockwell town in winter, and everybody talks about how wonderful it would be if the kids could just stay, but they all agree there's not really any work to speak of to keep a body fed and housed. The children can afford to lament because there really is no possibility of their staying. If there were, they'd have to come up with other reasons for leaving. And they all are ready to leave after three days. The first day, they settle in. The second day, they hit the high point of the visit. By the third day, they've remembered all the reasons they had to get out of there in the first place. The wisest plan their vacations to end at this point; the foolish stay the rest of the week.

Clara's Kitchen is open on Thanksgiving and Christmas — not all day, but from two to five in the afternoon. Stella makes the traditional dinner and serves it free to everyone over sixty who doesn't have family to dine with. Usually ten or fifteen folks show up. Used to be only four or five, but there's a couple of folks who have actually outlived their children now. Old Man Wright and his missus, whose two boys both died in the Vietnam War; Thelma Rickey, whose only daughter died of breast cancer. Then there's a couple of folks who had fallings out, you might say, with their offspring: the daughter disowned for marrying the wrong fellow, the son spurned because he took up the life of a traveling musician.

Then some years even the most loyal children are tied up elsewhere, appeasing in-laws who live in Minneapolis or Miami or Monterey. And a few who just plain and simple can't afford to make the trip back every year.

There's even two or three folks who never got married, never had children.

It was a clear and cold Christmas Eve in 1992. There hadn't been much snow at all that year. Stella always asked Ellie to help her, knowing that Ellie's family had all passed. Stella always invited Nadja and Granny, too, so Ellie wouldn't be the only relative youngster among the octogenarians. The Wrights, Amy Bickford, Wilma, Ida, Thelma, Maurice, Fred Thompson, Minnie, Lester and Helen — and a few others that weren't regulars, but Stella had heard of them through her annual phone calls to all the pastors and the chief of police. That's how she knew who needed her invitation. They either were known through the churches or because Denny Ellis had picked them up outside Pete's at closing time and taken them to jail to sleep off their drunk so they wouldn't freeze to death out there in the cold.

Helen agreed to come because Minnie was coming. Lester hoped it would do her a little good to get out. Besides, she never could cook a turkey worth a nickel. Couldn't even get a Jell-O salad right, when it came right down to it.

Because she didn't charge anything, Stella considered these gatherings parties. And so she presumed to serve beer and wine, even though she had no liquor license. Nobody minded. If you can't have a drink on the holidays, what makes it different from any other day?

Fred Thompson had a few such holiday drinks, and got a bug up his behind about Nadja. "Hey, missy," he called to her finally, from a table that was across the room from where Granny and Nadja sat. "Ain't you the one reads plates? Listen, sweetheart, I got this amazing plate over here. I can just tell it's got some special message for me on it. Whyn't you come over here and read it for me?" Nadja just smiled and said nothing at first, but Fred persisted. "What's this big hard thing on my plate, sweetheart? What does it mean?" he sniggered, waving the drumstick bone in the air. Fred never had had much social grace or charm, and any sense of propriety he did have was just about the first thing to go when he popped a beer or three and guzzled them down.

"Now, Fred, behave yourself, or I'll have to take you back home," Stella broke in, but it was Granny who finally put the stopper on. She whispered something to Nadja, then rose to her full four-foot, eleven-inch height and began to make her way across the room with the kind of steady determination that gave people time to be silent. Then some more time in which to attempt natural-sounding conversation, while keeping a covert eye and ear out so as not to miss the delicious confrontation they were sure was coming.

By the time Granny reached Fred's table, which he shared with the Wrights, everyone had given up the pretense and was simply watching and waiting.

Granny took her time settling into the fourth chair at the table. Then she finally spoke.

"Give me your left hand and I'll tell your fortune for you," she said.

"Why my left hand?" Fred asked.

"You're left-handed, ain't you?" A little murmur rolled around the room. Fred was left-handed. His nickname in high school had been Lefty. How did Granny know that?

Granny just kept her steady eye right on Fred and held out her hand. Fred was a little confused. He had just wanted to get a rise out of the little gal. Now here's this crone in his face wanting to read his palm. He wasn't exactly sure how he got from A to B. But Granny had him nailed now, and confused or no, he saw that indeed he was going to get his palm read. Something in her manner just sort of made it crystal-clear.

He held his left hand out and Granny grasped it. People at the other tables turned in their seats now, and craned their necks to unabashedly follow the action.

Granny traced a long crevice on Fred's hand. "Your life line is long," she said, still looking directly into his eyes, "but there is a break in the thirty-second year. I would say that perhaps you had an injury that year, is that true?"

Fred began to recover. He looked around the restaurant and nodded, like he was the guest on a TV talk show and these were his fascinated fans in the studio audience. "That must be my war wounds," he said, pleased to be able to remind everyone of his bravery, his service to his country.

Granny continued. "It's a strong line, and it goes on for a long time, but there is a weakness here, in the sixtieth year, that can cause problems."

"A weakness?" Fred didn't like that term at all. His wife had died the year he was sixty, but that was *her* weakness. He'd been strong. Still was strong, for a man his age. Hell, he could still buck bales if he had to.

"Someone close to you died," Granny went on, "and you stopped taking care of your health. You began to drink too much. Now your liver is affected. And your judgment."

Fred laughed. "You sound like Dr. Hanson," he said. "Is he paying you to say this?"

"You have too much beer to drink and it makes you think its all right to be rude to women."

"Now you sound like Reverend Johnson," Fred guffawed, trying his damnedest to sound amused and unaffected. "You ain't told my future yet, though." Fred winked at Old Man Wright, who gave him no visible response due to the fact that Mary Wright was keeping a sharp eye on all the proceedings, and Mary Wright never had thought terribly highly of Fred Thompson.

"Here's your future." Granny pointed to a dimple in Fred's palm. "You lay off the bottle or you'll be buried by Sunday."

This was a little strong for the old folks of Heaven. More than one of them gasped. Fred guffawed even more loudly than before. "Issat a promise?" he wanted to know.

"You don't have to die yet," Granny said sternly. "But you have to decide. You're a strong man and you could be doing some good in this world if you decide to do it. You could call your daughter and wish her a Merry Christmas."

"Now what the hell is that supposed to mean?" Fred exploded. If anyone in Clara's Kitchen hadn't been paying attention before, they surely paid it now. Seems Fred had told everyone twenty-one years before that his daughter Muriel had died, been taken by a sudden sickness after she moved to New York City. It was especially tragic because she'd just written to say she was engaged to a fellow who worked on Wall Street. Such a young woman, with so much to live for. Fred's wife Frieda had collapsed from the news and really never quite recovered. She was so grief-stricken it surely never would have occurred to anyone to wonder. Fred said Muriel was buried there before anyone got word back to them about what had happened. Can you imagine that? Those big-city bureaucrats don't have the sense they were born with — not even able to find the family in time for a decent funeral. And then Frieda just wasn't even up to traveling to pick up her things. Everyone agreed that was one of the most awful dangers to a child, especially a female child, going off to a big city like that, and so far away. To think a body could die and the family wouldn't even know for two weeks. Well, anyway, Frieda had just gone on and grieved herself to death and then Fred had started to drink and no one thought for a second that it was for any reason other than the logical one, namely the tragic death of their daughter.

But Granny wasn't finished. She was on a roll. "Open those letters," she said. "You know the ones I mean. Open them and read them, then call that girl of yours and ask her to forgive you. You don't need to come to Stella's next Christmas. You could have Christmas dinner with your own grandchildren."

Fred was stone-cold sober by now, and it was a lucky thing he did have a strong heart because otherwise it surely might have given out under the shock of it all. Granny had one more thing to say.

"It's a shame," she said, "When a child can't be loved. Nothing a child could do should ever stop a parent's love. But it's never too late, as long as you're living, to change things. You call her up. Otherwise, I'm afraid we're going to find you froze to death under two feet of ice and snow."

With these final portentous words, Granny released Fred's hand and gaze, stood, and pushed her chair back.

Old Man Wright peered at Fred, who sat rigid as a statue or a man who'd seen a ghost, which he pretty much had. "Well, Fred, is that true? Is your Muriel still alive?"

The only thing Fred could bring himself to say was, "Now see, she don't have any right to know that. That's the devil's business to know stuff like that about people."

Mary Wright nipped that one right in the bud. "Why, Fred Thompson," she chided. "It's God that knows the truth in our hearts, not the devil. You should get down on your knees and thank Him that He called you to task in time for you to do something about it."

Granny, back at the table next to Nadja, was drained. Nadja leaned in to her and whispered "How'd you know that?"

"Just a hunch," Granny whispered back, allowing one or two folks to hear, "and it wore me out." Wilma Porter stirred a spoonful of sugar into her coffee and kept her mouth shut.

"Okay, everybody." Stella's brassy voice rang out over the assembled and quieted the flutter of speculation and gossip. In the corner, Minnie was yelling at deaf Amy Bickford, trying to explain what had happened. "STILL ALIVE" hung in the air over the sudden silence of the rest of the room. Minnie heard herself bellow, blushed, and yelled "I'LL TELL YOU LATER!" into Amy's uncomprehending ear.

It was still. Outside the front window, a few flakes of snow were beginning to fall. Stella, noting that, said, "I know the weatherman said no snow for a week, but I've got a feeling this is gonna be a big one. Let's sing a few carols and then get you folks home. Helen, will you lead us?"

And Helen Breck's warbling soprano took off, leading the assembled in "Angels We Have Heard on High." She warbled a little more than usual, because she was struggling with what Granny had said about parents.

After "It Came Upon a Midnight Clear," "Joy to the World," and "Silent Night," the party broke up. The Wrights dropped Fred off at his house. Lester and Helen took Minnie home. Thelma lived just up the street, and Nadja and Granny walked her home. Stella piled the rest of the folks into her van.

By midnight there was a foot of snow on the ground and it was still falling. By Sunday morning, two feet had accumulated. There was a brief thaw, then the temperature fell to the teens, covering the town in a solid sheet of ice. No one could get around much except on the main roads, which were heavily salted, sanded, and scraped.

Old Man Wright tried to call Fred to see how he was doing, but the weight of the ice on the phone lines had caused them to snap. The sheriff heard the story from Dennis Ellis, who heard it from Seese, who heard it, of course, from Minnie, so it was hopelessly garbled. Something about a spell Granny had put on Fred, and Minnie wouldn't let it rest until Sheriff Underhill chained up and drove out to the Thompson house. Fred was nowhere to be found. His truck was missing, too. Old Man Wright said he was sure he had seen it Christmas night. That set the town to speculating about which ravine they'd find him in. There weren't too many, the land being as flat as it was. They figured he wouldn't drive into the bog because Granny said they'd find him, and nothing that went into the bog ever got found. Minnie told Seese to tell Dennis that Sheriff Underhill ought to arrest Granny for murder and witchcraft. Yes, Fred's disappearance caused quite a stir.

1993 came and there was still no sign of Fred. Someone finally got around to asking Granny what she thought. "He's a tough son-of-a-b," she said. "He'll be back." On the second Saturday in January, Fred's truck was sighted outside Clara's Kitchen. Inside, Fred was introducing his grandsons to Stella and Ellie. The boys, twelve and fifteen, were elbowing each other and snickering about the faded, stained signs on the wall. "Michael and Jeffrey," Fred said, "This is Stella and Ellie. Stell, Ellie, my grandsons Michael and Jeffrey Chen. They're gonna spend the weekend here and see where their ma grew up. You better feed 'em some lunch, Stell. You know I ain't cooked in my life, and I don't believe I'm gonna start now."

Back in the kitchen, Stella stood next to Ellie while they both chopped lettuce and tomatoes for the soup and salad special. "Well, I'll be," Stella breathed. "See, we heard Muriel met a fellow, but we never knew it was a Chinaman. Fred's dad was a Klokard, you know, and Fred grew up with those kind of notions."

"A Klokard?" Ellie asked.

"A speaker for the Klan," Stella whispered. "You know, back in the twenties they pretty much ran Heaven."

"How could they?"

"Well, they talked a lot about doing things for the community, you know. They put in that swing set over at the fairgrounds. Stuff like that. Your granddad was the Kleagle."

"What's that?"

"Why, the recruiter. He got pretty near everybody to sign up."

"That's what those books were!" Ellie stopped chopping and looked at Stella. "When Grandma Reba died and I cleared out the attic, there were all these ledgers with names in them. A lot of the family names in Heaven."

"All except the Catholics, I bet," grinned Stella. "They didn't let the Catholics join."

Ellie thought for a moment. "Well, there weren't any Flynns. I remember looking for them. How do you know so much about Heaven's history?"

"Oh, I was a secretary at the *Sentinel* back in '54. I typed up all the articles for the Centennial Committee. They found out a lot of interesting things about our history here. Didn't print some of it. There was some that said it was too controversial. The Historical Society put a lot of it together in a book."

"1954. That's the year I was born," Ellie said.

"Yep, you and Seese. You two were our Centennial babies. And Melinda was our Centennial death."

"Lester's daughter?"

"Yep. Right at the end of the Centennial Fair. I've got the book in a closet somewhere. I'll bring it in for you to look at."

"Hey, Stell. You cutting that lettuce or growing it from seed?" came Fred's roar from the front.

"Oh, hush up. We're getting it."

"See, boys, that's the pace of life in Heaven," Fred nodded solemnly. "You order your lunch, and if you're lucky you might get served sometime after the sun goes down."

"Don't take your manners from your granddad," Stella warned the boys as she put the salads on the table, "'cause he doesn't have any. So where are you boys from?"

. . .

A brick walk led to the little cottage. Each brick was laid at an angle to the next, and had an eight-pointed star motif baked in. Near the roots of an aging sycamore, where the ground heaved to accommodate new growth, many of the bricks were cracked and crumbled. It was a walkway that would terrify a child raised on rhymes about breaking your mother's back by stepping on a crack.

Maybe the house itself isolated its residents. Whatever the reasons, Granny and Nadja rarely had callers, except for Ellie. Like Cecil Moser and Charlene before them, they were left pretty much to themselves. Oh, people talked to them when they were downtown at Clara's, or shopping, or when Nadja was reading their plates. They just didn't drop by this house, nor telephone. So it was a surprise when one morning the phone did ring. It was Helen Breck, asking to speak to Mrs. White. "I won't waste your time beating around the bush," said Helen. "I'd like you to come over to Minnie Kelso's. There's something I have to talk to you about. Can you come right away?"

The old woman nodded yes to the phone, and as she wrote down the address, a few tears traced their way through the wrinkles in her weathered face. This was a call she'd been waiting for.

"You've been here in Heaven before." Helen wasn't asking a question.

"We were here in 1963," Granny said.

"And?" Helen hated to waste time. While she waited for Granny's answer she pulled a thick manila envelope from her bag.

"And 1954," Granny allowed. Then: "Are you the one who left her?"

There was a long, thick pause. Finally, Helen spoke again. "I don't want Lester to know yet. I'll tell him in my own good time. When can I meet with her? I have some legal papers for her, and some photographs of her mother."

1　9　9　4

· ·

SEESE TURNED OVER IN BED, away from Dennis and his heavy breath. She squinted at the alarm clock. It was six o'clock. In thirty minutes the hysterical chirping of the alarm would begin, like a wounded and frantic bird. She would roll out of bed carefully and quickly, to avoid disturbing Dennis, who currently worked the night shift. She would pad down the hall in the fuzzy yellow slippers the boys got her for Christmas last year. She disliked yellow, but Ned had this notion it was cheerful, so they bought yellow in the hopes that their mother's morning disposition might be improved by it.

She didn't like Dennis being on the night shift. It meant, for one thing, that she'd had to give up her Wednesday evening hours at the shop, because even though he couldn't watch them now, he forbade her to hire a babysitter. Dennis didn't believe in them. He felt that much of the trouble in the world, or at least in this country, stemmed from parents, most specifically mothers, being out of the home. Seese agreed with him up to a point. But since the boat they took to the lake each summer came from her earnings, and since the college fund did too, and since their ability to move into their new split-level out on Oak Lane, where the boys had safe bicycle routes and plenty of grassy fields in which to toss their footballs and hit their baseballs, and most importantly, a paved patio that was large enough for not just one but two basketball hoops, so that it was almost a regulation-sized court — since all these things were possible in part due to her income, Seese had the temerity to think that it was reasonable for her to keep one evening a week available to her clients.

Dennis had cut her short with an "I'm not going to discuss this anymore." He was a policeman, and used to being the authority. "You will not work on evenings that I work."

What was most difficult for Seese was the suspicion that nibbled at her peace of mind. It occurred to her in the corners of her awareness that Dennis never used to be like this. It occurred to her that if she were out on Wednesday night she might see something or hear something to make her doubt his loyalty.

It had been more than four months — when Denny's schedule had changed — since they had made love.

Not that sex was a frequent event anyway. Seese and Dennis were both members of Caring for Life, and both agreed that abortion was murder. And Dennis believed as well that birth control was immoral. Procreation was the purpose of sex for Dennis, and after the birth of their fourth son, he announced that they'd had more than their share. He instructed Seese to never again expect him to touch her sexually. But every once in a while he seemed to have forgotten this order, or at least he felt free to expect sex when he wanted it, which was usually on Monday nights during football season. Seese didn't mind. In fact, she looked forward to these nights. She halfway hoped for another pregnancy — for a baby girl — a child that might care about some of the things she cared about. After these Monday-night episodes, Dennis would seem even more withdrawn for a while, usually not warming up again until he saw the wrappers in the bathroom trash that assured him she was having a period, and not another baby.

What bothered Seese almost as much as, or perhaps even more than, Dennis's withdrawal of physical contact and affection was the specter of Heaven's denizens knowing that there was trouble in her marriage. Seese had made it her business now for over twenty years to know the business of everyone else in Heaven. She did not want this particular relationship to be mutual. Like Charlene before her, Seese wanted her secrets to stay secret. Not that her secrets were shocking and perverse like Charlene's. Nevertheless, she would lose power if people knew her secrets, and Seese did not want to lose power.

But no one can contain their griefs and confusions without some outlet. A person will place a long-distance call, write to Ann or Abby, even talk in their sleep if they have to, just to let some of the pressure out. Seese found her vent in keeping a journal. As a child, she'd always kept a locked diary, the kind with the tiny key that opens any locked diary made by the same company. In her teens she kept the kind that had popular teenage cartoon characters draped over each page, saying typical teenage things.

When Seese married Dennis she gave up the diaries. She didn't need diaries with Dennis there to talk to. And they felt so much the same way about things. When the babies began to be born, there wasn't even time to keep a diary, between keeping the shop open and the boys fed and dry.

Now, on Wednesday nights, she had time to write down her thoughts. Ned was working at Boyd's Happy Burgers till ten, and usually went straight to bed when he got home. Chip and Sam did homework for an hour after dinner, and then were permitted to watch TV till bedtime. Mel was absorbed in his Nintendo. Dinners got simpler on Wednesdays, as on all nights, since Dennis wasn't home anyway. Hot dogs, macaroni and cheese, and pizzas began to replace the oven-baked chicken and pot roasts Dennis liked.

Seese confided her worries to her journal, a bound black book that was actually supposed to be a sketch book. It had nice big pages that she filled with her careful script.

On this particular morning, she had no customers scheduled until eleven o'clock, so after the boys were all packed off to school, Seese drove in to her shop, set the sign on the door to say "Back at 10:30," and walked over to Clara's Kitchen for a second cup of coffee. She took the back booth and pressed herself against the wall so other customers wouldn't see her and expect conversation. She took her journal out and wrote about her obsession. What is she like, I wonder, Seese wrote. What does she do to him in bed? Does she use birth control? What does her hair look like? What does he say to her? What does he think of when we're sitting next to each other in church? What has he promised her? Seese was pretty sure, knowing Dennis, that he hadn't promised her anything, but she wrote the question down. What is her name? Where does she live? Does she know who I am? And suddenly a sickening idea reared its ugly head. Does she come in to my shop? Seese closed the journal. It was too much to contemplate.

Ellie came by just then with the bottomless coffeepot, and Seese said, "Bring me one of those cinnamon rolls, too." Then she ate the roll slowly, picking out all the raisins and arranging them in small circles around the edge of her plate. When Ellie came with a third refill Seese realized that it was after 10:30. "I gotta get over to the shop," she said, and jumped up. Her journal of anguished suspicions lay behind on the table next to the wall.

Ellie saw it there, but said nothing. After Seese left, she picked it up as she wiped the table down, then slipped it into her purse. On her break, she read it in the toilet stall. Then she put it in a brown bag with Seese's name on it. "If she doesn't come to pick it up," she told Stella, "I'll take it on over there when I'm off."

After the day Ellie showed up with Seese's journal a strange bond formed between them. Seese never directly asked Ellie if she had read the journal, and Ellie never directly admitted she had, but they began to discuss the ways of men and small towns with a rapport they'd never before had.

"Doncha wish you could figure out how to live without men altogether?" Seese asked Ellie suddenly one day, when there was no one else in the shop and she was running the clippers up the back of Ellie's neck to cut the hairs that strayed away from the hairline there.

"Oh, I don't know," said Ellie. "I think men can be all right. Sometimes."

"Oh, yeah, there's a few decent fellows around, I guess. Seems like most of 'em are either too old for us or too young for us, though."

"Age doesn't make that much difference," Ellie replied, and Seese was tantalized. Was this an admission that she and Lester were really doing it? Could a man as old as Lester really be a good lover?

"I s'pose they know better how to treat you," theorized Seese. "If they're smart enough to have learned anything during their lives."

"You know what I think the problem is?" Ellie offered. "I think it's when they get to thinking how important they are — like the world can't go on spinning without them." Though she didn't say so, Ellie had Dennis and his brother in mind as perfect examples. "I think the best man is a humble man. One who realizes he's just part of a big picture, like the rest of us, instead of thinking he's the damn painter all of the time."

Seese laughed. "Dennis is a painter," she said. "Or at least he thinks he is. He's got me painted into a corner."

Ellie waited. She knew Seese, having gone this far, would go on without prompting, and that her job was to appear almost disinterested, to make room for whatever revelation Seese was hatching out here.

"Yeah," Seese finally went on, as she turned the blow dryer on and began to comb out Ellie's hair, "he doesn't want me working Wednesday nights. 'Cause he's on the night shift and doesn't believe in babysitters. 'Course, Ned could watch 'em, but he works till ten. Denny says that the work experience is very valuable to Ned. Teaches him how to handle money. I said it doesn't make sense. I make more on a Wednesday night than Ned makes all week. But Denny…"

Seese broke off, hearing the bell over the door. In the mirror she saw Minnie reflected, negotiating her way in.

"Seese," Minnie said. "Do you have time for a shampoo? I don't know, I did something to my back and it hurts like the dickens to bend over the tub to wash my hair."

Seese spoke to the mirror image. "Come on in, Minnie. We're just about done here." She caught Ellie's eye and the smallest smile passed between the two of them.

. . .

Ellie was getting the first permanent of her entire life. Now that something had opened up between her and Seese, she found herself making excuses to schedule trips to the House of Beauty. She was amazed at Seese's encyclopedic knowledge of Heaven's business. Today Seese was letting Ellie in on la crème de la crème: her theory about Helen Breck. One she had not even shared with her own husband, or with Minnie.

"She told me once. Now, she didn't come right out and say it, but she really did tell. She let me know. 'Course, I always did know there was something more to it." Ellie waited. Seese moved behind the chair and got distracted with dribbling chemicals on Ellie's curlers. For a time, there was only the squish of the squeeze bottle and the sound of Seese's somewhat labored breathing.

Ellie wondered if she dared ask her to continue. But finally, without prompting, Seese resumed her monologue.

"I think she did something with that baby." Ellie looked at their reflections — caught Seese's eye, silently inquired. Seese went on, warming to her subject. "I think that baby was born right here in Heaven," she said. "They always said she must've left it in the Greyhound station up in Chicago, but I'll tell you what. I did a little research one time when I was up there. I went to the library downtown and looked through the microfilm of the *Chicago Tribune* for the whole month of August 1954, and I never found anything in it about a baby in a bus terminal. I subscribe to it, you know. They have to mail it to me, so the news is always two or three days late, but it's okay. I get to read up on Sunday, it's a kind of professional thing, you know. It gives me things to talk about with my customers. I get *USA Today*, too, and *Time*. Plus the *Indianapolis Star*, of course."

Again, she lapsed to silence, while she set the timer for fourteen minutes. "Let me know if it starts to burn before that," she said. You've got such fair skin, it might." Then she busied herself sweeping hair clippings. Ellie waited, then prompted. "Is that the sort of thing you'd see in the *Chicago Tribune*?"

"Oh, yes," Seese assured her. They have a local section and a police beat section. You see all kinds of stories in those sections. You know, there was that case just about a month ago, where that young girl left her baby in that service-station restroom? Remember?"

Ellie demurred. She had not heard the story before.

"See, that was a story I read in the *Tribune*. I like the *Tribune* because it's a respectable paper," she said. "I know I can trust what I read there. Not like *The National Enquirer*. Now, that paper is just trash. Ridiculous trash. I don't see why so many people want to buy it. Don't they have anything better to do with their time but read silly stuff about two-headed-monster babies, or people seeing Elvis in an old tree stump or something? And those television shows. Can you imagine going on those things and hanging up your dirty laundry for the whole world to see? Nosir. Not me."

"What did she tell you?" Ellie couldn't abide any more indirect setup. But Seese busied herself straightening curlers and combs and acted like she hadn't heard the question. Then she moved on to the magazines.

Ellie wondered if the burning she felt on her scalp was bad enough to remark on. She decided to wait on that, and put forth another question. "Do they know where she went? The daughter? I heard she never went to her aunt's house."

"Oh, well, that's what they say, but it sounds a little fishy to me. I mean, I think the aunt was part to blame. Kicked her out when she came due, so she wouldn't get stuck raising the baby, and then lied about it after so she wouldn't be accused of negligence or something. The girl did mail letters home from Iowa. Minnie said she saw them, saw the dates on them. Helen used to carry them all with her, oh, she musta done that for four or five years before she settled down to serious grieving."

"Serious grieving?"

"You know what I mean. The way she went all crazy for a while. You know she used to think Lester was dead."

"Yeah, I do remember hearing that."

"But one time, just after she decided he was alive after all, she was in here talking about Melinda and she said something about the missing baby, and she called it a 'her.'"

"So she knew what sex it was?"

Seese looked triumphant. With an expression full of smug significance, she pronounced, "Sure sounds like it to me."

"Hmmm," was about all Ellie could think of to say.

"But she seems to be doing pretty well these days."

"Uh-huh."

"She's coming in here asking all kinds of questions about beauty products. She even got a manicure last week. That's something, isn't it? At the age of seventy-something, to suddenly start taking care of your appearance?"

Ellie was quiet, busy putting two and two together.

• • •

"Today's topic," the talk-show host proclaimed, is 'Abandoned Babies: Who Are They? Who Leaves Them?'"

Lester reached for the remote control, but Helen stopped him. "Leave it on," she said. "I want to hear it."

"Don't you think it might just upset you, Mother?"

"Leave it on."

"Well, all right."

The talk shows had become a ritual at the Breck house. Every afternoon after lunch, Helen turned on the TV and watched for three hours straight. She had become fascinated, you might even say obsessed, with how willingly people told everything about themselves right there on national television.

Lester kind of liked them, too. He'd always felt a little guilty about his extramarital escapades, but the stories he heard on Geraldo made him feel positively saintly. But this one — he wasn't sure it was going to make him feel at all better.

They watched for a while in silence while the guests introduced themselves, but when one of the members of the studio audience said she thought any woman that could abandon a baby would surely burn in hell, Helen got up abruptly.

"It's easy to judge," soothed Lester. "No one knows what a person really goes through."

Helen looked at him wordlessly, then crossed to the rolltop desk. She pulled the bottom drawer all the way out. From the very back, she took out an old cigar box. From the box, she took a letter. She crossed back to Lester, stood in front of him and held it out. "Read this," she said.

Lester took the letter. "What is it?"

"Just read it."

Lester looked at the address. Originally mailed to Helen's childhood home, it had been forwarded. He recognized the spidery handwriting of Alma Porter, postmistress until her daughter Wilma assumed the job back in '78. He pulled the pages from the envelope and began to read aloud, "Dear Miss Tipton."

Helen interrupted: "Read it to yourself."

The letter, dated January 1954, was from a Reverend Whitney Trout in Columbus, Ohio. "It is my unhappy duty," the Reverend Trout wrote, "to inform you of the recent death of your father, Abraham Hartley." Lester looked up, questioning.

"I was adopted," Helen said.

"I never knew that."

"I know. Read the letter."

As his pastor and confidante, I guaranteed your father before his death that I would carry out his wish that I contact you to tell you that he never forgot you, nor your mother. He has kept you in his heart and hopes that you can forgive him for his inability to care for you better.

*As you probably know, your mother Jenny Saultmeier
Hartley brought you and your brother James to your
current town of residence in 1924. Your father was to
follow, from Terre Haute, soon thereafter. Unfortunately,
he was arrested for attempting to gain free passage on
a freight train, and detained in the Terre Haute jail for
sixty days. It was during these days that God saw fit to
take your dear mother and her eldest child, your brother.
When Abraham arrived in Heaven and inquired about
his family, he was told that Jenny and James had both
died from influenza and that you had been taken in by
a family named Tipton. It was further suggested to him
that he would be well advised to leave Heaven before
sundown without trying to see you, upon pain of death,
which advice he took.*

*He made his way to Columbus, where he met and
married his second wife, who bore him five children.
He worked hard to provide them with a good life, and
died last Saturday of a heart attack, leaving three grandchildren as well.*

*I trust the enclosed photograph will explain more
directly than I can why Abraham never felt that he could
contact you during his life.*

*Rest assured, Miss Tipton, that your father was a
god-fearing and decent man, who held you in his hopes
and prayers every day of his life.*

*With sincere best wishes for your good health and
happiness,*

Reverend Whitney Trout

Lester looked in the envelope for the picture referred to.
"What happened to it?" he asked Helen.

"I burned it," she said. "A long time ago."

"Why?"

"They were all colored."

"What?"

"They were all colored. My father was colored. By himself you would hardly be able to tell, but next to his wife and children — "

"Nawwww..."

Helen was crying, and it frightened Lester. In five decades of marriage, he had never seen her cry.

"This letter came a month before Melinda...before that hateful man came through here and ruined our lives. I was so afraid the baby would be dark. I couldn't...I just couldn't...And then when I saw her...all that curly dark hair..." Helen was unable to go on.

"Mother, Mother, hush now." Lester put the letter aside and stood to face Helen. "It's all right. It's all right." He took her hands in his and they stood there, weeping with each other: two old people with more sorrow than anyone ought rightly have to bear. Behind them, on the television set, the camera panned the faces of Sandi's six guests. Every one of them had tears in their eyes.

• • •

In the barn, he talks with the pigs. He tells them everything. How she got herself knocked up by that snake of a salesman, how the missus sent her out to the barn, just about exactly the same spot he now sat in. How it was he who had brought her the news and her meals, and rubbed her feet the way he'd once rubbed his wife's feet when they got so swollen in her pregnancy. How it was he who had delivered the tiny thing, cut the cord. How he was so embarrassed at first to view his own daughter so closely, so intimately. How it was easier than delivering cows. How he should have called the doctor. How the missus was in shock. How she cracked under the strain. How he should have stopped her. How he wished he'd known.

He weeps with the pigs. He weeps for his dead daughter. Her young farm-fresh face comes back to him, over and over, dancing in his barnyard like the cut-off head of a Sunday-dinner chicken. Her mouth opens and closes silently, and her head bounces around the barnyard. At times he feels the only way to stop it is to kill, but he can't figure out who or what to kill. He weeps for his wife. For her stern unhappy life, lived under the shadow of her fear. For her grief, for her bitter guilt. He weeps for himself. For the life that has passed by with so little to show for it. Childless life, loveless life. Life wasted in ignorance, bound by fear. Life drowned in thousands of thoughtless cups of coffee and dozens of foolish liaisons while the truth lay coiled like a copperhead by the woodpile, waiting to strike him in his old age.

Then it happens, the way things so often seem to happen — foolishly. He falters, and feels the sudden sharp pain travel down his arm. Attempting to steady himself, he slips in manure, falls on a squealing pig, grabs at the boards of the pigsty and misses. As he hits the barn floor struggling for breath, he considers that this is what his life has come to: dying in pig shit, without a shred of dignity. He closes his eyes, sucks his painful breaths, and waits. Then everything goes black.

The first thing he sees when he wakes up is the line — the red line graphing its way across the screen on the box by the bed. It is almost straight, but every now and then a small blip appears in it. First to the up side, then to the down side. It takes a few moments for him to suspect that it is his heart he is watching. When the anxious thought strikes him that the line is too nearly straight for health and comfort, it jumps.

He wants to go home, but there are tubes in every conceivable place, and he is too weak to lift his head from the pillow, let alone stand and walk. It comes to him slowly that he is not dead, that he is not in the pigsty, that something of which he has absolutely no recollection has happened in his life.

It alarms him. Then again, maybe he *is* dead. But heaven doesn't monitor hearts, does it? Unless maybe the devil...

He falls asleep again, dreams of his pregnant daughter. She is giving birth. He is there. Flustered. Boiling water in the chicken coop. But when he takes it to her it is Ellie he sees, and behind her stands that Gypsy girl Nadja, challenging him, and he knows that Nadja has killed Melinda. But he doesn't know what has happened to the baby. Frantically, he begins to dig through the straw. He feels something, pulls it up. It is a doll's cloth body, porcelain hands, feet and neck, and a large hook with eyeballs on the end where its head should be. *Mama*, it cries, blinking its headless eyes. *Mama*. He wakes gasping, sucking in air like a man who's come close to drowning. The dream is gone but the terror remains. Undefined terror. The red blips hurry across the monitor, the door opens, and the night nurse rushes in. She looks like Nadja. He shakes his head. No, she doesn't. She is the Tremaine girl, that lives across the alley from Maurice's.

"You doin' okay?" Her voice is honey-sweet and so smooth. "Let me take your pulse. We better double-check this." And she grasps his wrist between her thumb and fingers. The touch calms him. He watches the monitor slow down, feels the gentle pressure on his wrist, and aches.

"Where's Helen?" he asks, but she acts like she hasn't heard.

"You just rest now," the girl coos. "You're doing just fine." And she flutters out of the room.

. . .

"Isn't the sky spectacular tonight? That clean, straight line of horizon, and above it it's like an inspired painter's canvas — all that blue and gold and pink. I used to sit in the front yard and watch skies like this. And after a while the blues would go grey, and the pinks would wisp away and the golds would settle below, behind the edge of the earth, and the owl would come out. He — or she — but I always thought of it as a he — always sat on the next-to-the-lowest branch of the maple tree in our front yard. And if I watched long enough, I'd see him swoop, suddenly and silently, to catch some oblivious mouse who thought it was safe to go out. Sometimes there'd be a small surprised squeak. Sometimes the owl would call out. My grandma hated that. She said it meant someone died.

And it was true. Every time we heard the owl, it wouldn't be but a day or two and we'd hear about someone dying. But I saw an owl tonight in the tree by the emergency entrance. And it didn't make a sound. So I think he's going to make it."

"You're a poet, you know that?" said the man from Detroit, whose father was recuperating from surgery in the room next to Lester.

Ellie laughed. "I just get carried away with words sometimes. Not often, really."

"Have you had anything to eat today?"

"No, just this awful coffee. Why do they give us this dreadful stuff, when the Golden Guernsey Dairy Farm is right next door?" Nevertheless, she tore open a pack of powdered creamer and added it to the sugar she had just stirred into her cup.

The man from Detroit smiled at her. "Let me buy you dinner."

"When are you heading back home?"

"First thing in the morning."

"There's not too much exciting near here. Let's go over to Marion. I heard there's a good new Italian restaurant opened up there."

. . .

Lester Breck remembers when his Dad told him about John Dillinger robbing the bank over in Montpelier. He remembers how excited his father and mother had been — making him come inside from the yard because they were afraid the famous outlaw was going to come through Heaven, turn off Creek onto Millstone, tear up the long driveway and kidnap little Lester. Lester was far too young to know how truly irrational this fear was. He absorbed it all as extremely likely, in fact. When Dillinger was captured, it didn't change things. Lester still expected the outlaw to roar up the driveway, leap out of his car, and grab him. He expected to be thrown into the trunk of the car and driven to a secret place. He expected to be fed peanut butter on saltines. He expected he would be given only water to drink — certainly not the good rich milk he loved, that came thick and warm from Gert, their guernsey. Lester expected that he would never see his mother and father again. He expected to be kept in an underground chamber of some kind, maybe a root cellar.

At night when Lester's mother put him to bed, he began to want the lamp left on. Lester's mother was an indulgent woman, so she allowed him to have his way. After he finally fell asleep, she would quietly step back into his room and turn the wick down.

After a few months, he outgrew his night terrors and learned to tolerate the dark. What happened was, his cousin Will came to spend the night, when Will's mother had to stay a spell in the hospital. That was when her twin girls were born. Will was a year older than Lester, and he wasn't afraid of anything. Lester didn't want to let on to Will that he ordinarily went to sleep with his lamp on. Besides, with Will there in the room with him on the rollaway bed, Lester really didn't feel afraid. So when his mother came to say good night, Lester said, "don't forget to turn down the lamp," and they both knew it would be okay from then on.

Will was the first man from Heaven to enlist after Pearl Harbor, and Lester was the second. Will got sent to Europe; Lester was stationed in India. Will fought bravely, lost a leg, was captured and taken to a POW camp in Poland; he escaped, was recaptured, escaped again, and made his way to a barn near the Baltic Sea, where he was trying to figure out how to get to Sweden when VE Day was declared.

Lester played bridge.

Will never held it against Lester that it turned out that way. That's the kind of family theirs was. Accepting and forgiving. Will died in 1987 at sixty-nine after getting a severe case of food poisoning at a hamburger stand near Valparaiso. He had been on his way back from visiting his son and daughter-in-law.

He stands at a crossroads and sees Will standing in a field to the right. Will is shaking his head silently, discouraging Lester. At Will's side, Lester sees Melinda, pretty as ever, and now here comes Helen, who walks right by him to join the other two. She doesn't even notice Lester, and when she reaches her daughter, all three of them turn and walk away. Darned if his mother and father aren't there, too. Lester wants to follow them, but there is something about the left turn that pulls at him.

He drifts out of his dream, wakes up to rediscover the plastic tubes still threaded through his nose and down his throat. An IV bottle hangs at his bedside, dripping something into his veins through a needle stuck in the back of his left hand. His body hurts like hell, but he can't tell exactly where the pain is. And someone is sitting by his side.

"You had a good long nap," Ellie says. "We were wondering when you'd get around to waking up."

Lester peers at her. "Now, who are you?" Ellie leans in so he can see her better.

"It's Ellie," she says.

A slight smile registers on Lester's lips. "Ellie," he repeats.

She is suddenly terribly afraid of what he might ask next. "Now that you're awake," she hurries on, "I'd better let the nurses know." She pats his free hand and walks quickly from the room.

. . .

"I don't believe she's here." Minnie's sotto voice cautioned Ida Tipton to wait a moment. Then Minnie turned and glanced back casually to note that Ellie and Nadja had taken seats in the last pew.

"Which one?" Ida breathed carefully. She would have been surprised to see either of them there.

"Why, Ellie Denson." Minnie leaned into Ida's ear so she could go into some detail. "You know she and Lester were carrying on together." Ida's eyes widened. She hadn't known. Actually, Minnie hadn't known either, but she'd always suspected. Her way of confirming her theory was to put it out and see if anyone else already knew. Minnie lived with the constant suspicion that life passed her by, that she was always the last to be let in on things.

Ida lived with the constant fear that she would appear silly and stupid to others. To cover the fact that she was utterly amazed by Minnie's revelation, she nodded.

"Come to think of it," Ida lied, "I did hear something to that effect. She's got some nerve, if it's true," she added, so as not to commit the sin of false accusation.

Having secured her position on that exchange, Ida was able to admit to being baffled by another item. "That Gypsy woman didn't know Helen, did she?"

Now Minnie was in her glory. She really did know something that no one else knew.

"As a matter of fact, Helen saw her a few times in secret." Minnie held her hand casually over her mouth to keep the exchange private.

"You don't say!" Ida exclaimed softly.

"I do say," Minnie rejoined, triumphantly but quietly. "It was my house she saw her in. Well, she was so sick and tired of everybody pitying her so, she knew if she went down to Stella's the whole town'd be leaning over her shoulder. And she went over to Charlene's house once, but she said it reminded her too much of the day she found...." Millie faltered briefly, searching for the right pronoun. "Anyway," she continued, she asked Miss Nadja and Miss Nancy to meet her at my house, where there wouldn't be any nosy neighbors. Made me promise to keep it a secret. Don't you breathe a word of it, now. Even if she is dead, she deserves to have her wishes respected."

"Don't you worry," Ida assured her, mentally listing people to whom she might impart this gem without truly violating

Helen's desire for secrecy. After all, it couldn't hurt her now. And there were so few occasions where Ida was this close to the source of news. She might never again have the opportunity to be the first to tell something to someone.

Then the organist began to play a slow and stately version of "Shall We Gather at the River" and Minnie gave Ida a sign to hush, which Ida resented because she knew better than to talk during the service and didn't like being treated like a child when she was well into her seventies and, truth be known, two years older than Minnie. Always had been, always would be.

The next Tuesday morning, Minnie went for her now bi-weekly shampoo and styling. Seese worked the lather through Minnie's thinning hair and put the question to her. "What's this I hear about Helen and that Gypsy woman holding seances over at your house? What were they trying to do, raise the dead granddaughter?"

Minnie's eyes flew open, then shut again as the stinging soap ran in.

"Who told you that? Ida?"

"No, Ida didn't tell me. I heard it from Dennis. He said Tyler told him."

"Tyler Wanamaker? Now, how would he know anything at all about Helen?"

"Well, his sister-in-law's mother is a next-door neighbor of Lucy Namsell, and she goes over there to First United. She got it from Wilbur Warner. He was one of the pallbearers, wasn't he?"

Seese always knew her sources. She didn't always share them, but she always knew them. She rinsed the soap from Minnie's head and worked conditioner through her hair as Minnie struggled in her mind to sort out the leak. Was Wilbur sitting behind them at the funeral? Did Ida tell Wilbur? Did the Gypsy tell? Had Helen told someone other than Minnie? This last possibility pained her so much she rejected it out of hand.

Out loud she said only, "'Twasn't any seance. She just had her plate read like anyone else that goes down there to Stella's."

Seese rubbed the terrycloth towel briskly over Minnie's scalp, then made a turban of it. "All set," she said, leading Minnie to the chair. As she gathered her clips and combs, she asked, as casually as she would ask if the mail had come yet on a day when she knew it was all going to be junk mail, "Did she find anything out?"

"Oh, I don't know," said Minnie. "Miss Nadja always wanted them to be alone, so I never heard much of what they said. 'Course, it's a small house, you know, and a person can't help but overhear a few things."

Seese nodded and removed the towel. "Do you want a little trim today, too? Looks like a few of these hairs are splitting."

"If you think I should," Minnie said. "You're the expert on splitting hairs."

And as Seese clipped and snipped, Minnie continued reporting.

"No, I didn't hear too much. Something about Moses once, and one time I heard the old lady tell her, 'There is no power on earth can keep you from your granddaughter when you're meant to find her.' So see, that's where she got the notion that it was a girl."

"What do you think?" Seese asked.

"I think it looks fine," Minnie said, examining her hair length in the large mirror.

"No, I mean about the Gypsy. You think she told Helen anything worthwhile? You think she knew anything?"

"Well, Helen sure took it like she did," Minnie exclaimed. "She tried to give her some money — I mean quite a lot, too, but Miss Nadja wouldn't take it.

"And she told Helen to forgive herself. Now, what do you suppose that was about? Helen did everything she could to find that baby. What would she have to forgive herself about?"

"No telling," Seese said, "but whatever it was, she's forgiven now, rest her soul."

Minnie nodded, surprised by the sudden tears that sprang to her eyes. "Amen to that," she said, and the silence that settled for a while in Sue Ellen Sue's House of Beauty felt almost holy.

. . .

"How's Les doing?" Stella spooned oatmeal into Walter's mouth, and watched Ellie make her rounds of setting out the salt and pepper shakers.

"He's up and down." Ellie looked tired, and Stella was worried about her. "It really hurts him that he couldn't go to the funeral. They didn't even tell him about her stroke until he was out of ICU, and that was three days after she was buried. Minnie kept a scrapbook of the funeral for him, so at least he could see who'd been there and whatnot. Minnie was just about Helen's only friend I think, there towards the last."

"She's a good soul, that Minnie." Stella nodded to emphasize her thought.

"Yes, she is," Ellie agreed. "And with Lester in ICU and nobody knowing if he was going to live or die, well, she just sort of naturally stepped in and made the arrangements. She was actually going to have it videotaped, but the fellow she called that videotapes weddings said he didn't do funerals. Didn't think it was dignified, he told her. Then Dennis Ellis was going to do it for her but he got called to work overtime. Then somebody thought of the high school, but Minnie said she didn't think someone that young should do it. So in the end she just had Audrey Switzer take a couple of photos and then she pressed some of the flowers and had a little notebook next to the guest register where people could write something nice about Helen. Then she put the program and flowers and guest list and all that together in a scrapbook and brought it up to Lester."

Stella had finished feeding Walter and was setting up the cash register. Ellie was on to brewing coffee. "How much longer are they going to keep him?"

"Just a couple days more, I guess."

"Will he go out to the Westwind, then, till he can come home?"

"Well, he doesn't really want to go out there. He's anxious to get back home."

"Who'll take care of him? Surely he's not up to doing everything for himself. And Minnie's not that strong these days, either."

"I thought I could stay out there for a while."

Stella's eyebrows shot up. "That'll give folks something to talk about!"

Ellie looked bone-weary. "You know what, Stell? Let them talk. If Les wants to go home, I'm going to do what I can to help him."

"Tea, Walter?" Stella held a cup to her husband's lips and he slurped the warm liquid. "I guess I know what you mean. I'm not ready to see Walter in a nursing home. It always seems like once folks go in there they have a heck of a time ever getting out again. If Les wants to go home..." she paused for a moment and looked embarrassed. "Listen, Ell, I don't know quite how to say this, but if you do stay out there with him, do me a favor."

"What's that?"

"Make up the guest bed downstairs, and make sure it gets slept in." Stella caught Ellie's eye, and a tired smile passed between them.

"I will, counselor. Thanks. In fact, I'll give guided tours to anyone who wants to come and check for themselves."

Stella was serious. "It's way too soon for Lester to be thinking about anything besides getting well anyway."

Ellie nodded, and crossed to the door to flip the sign to 'Open.' No one was waiting to come in.

. . .

Helen Breck's will gave the slow and somewhat bored town something even more to talk about. There were only four people at the reading, which was held in Lester's hospital room at County, but it took less than a day for the news to spread to most of Heaven.

The will, dated April 7, 1955, had been drawn up by an attorney from Indianapolis. It declared, of course, that Helen was of sound mind and body, and everyone agreed that back in 1955 she was still of sound mind, and had always been of sound body. That is, up until she died. Yes, in 1955 Helen was still quite lucid, and what now set Heaven to serious gossiping is that in that year, she designated that her estate pass to her granddaughter, should the girl ever be found.

This was the first time anyone other than Seese had heard that Helen even knew the gender of the missing child. Everyone had a hypothesis. Most had figured that Melinda made a dying confession to her mother and told her she'd delivered a girl. Others wondered if Helen might have found a journal, or a note amidst Melinda's belongings.

It was perhaps strange that no one considered for an instant that Lester might know more about it than he'd let on. The assumption was that if there'd been secrets kept, they'd been between mother and daughter. Besides, there was already plenty to ask Lester about. Did he know that she owned the whole place? No, he didn't believe he did know that. Wasn't he going to challenge the will? Well, it looked like he'd have enough to live on. No, as long as he could stay in the house, he didn't believe there was any reason to sue. He always did say that he'd have gone bankrupt a long time ago if it hadn't been for Helen managing all the business. Didn't she get it all paid off by 1949? Some years he mostly wasn't even there, just Dad and Helen. He did remember that they'd had a party and tore up the old mortgage papers and set fire to them.

So now it turned out that Lester hardly owned the clothes on his back. The property was still on the tax rolls as jointly held, but an unregistered deed of trust clearly gave Helen sole ownership of the farm and acreage. The deed of trust was dated December 17, 1954. Maybe he did sign everything over to her then. Hard to remember, but it surely was his signature on the papers. Helen would never forge his signature, although there were many times that the business required him to sign on dotted lines. He always just signed whenever Helen said to.

Helen had set up a trust fund the next year, 1955, and each year, sane or round the bend, she had deposited money to this account. The amounts varied from year to year, and Helen could have told them why. She always placed eighty percent of the year's profits in the trust fund. Some years it was several thousand, other years, when there had been droughts or floods or late springs or early frosts, it was hardly ten dollars. The net result, nonetheless, was impressive. No one had ever had any idea that Helen Breck had salted away so much money.

The trust was set up in such a way that should Lester outlive Helen, he would receive the interest income. It was administered through a bank in Indianapolis. Upon Lester's death, the bank would include any remaining funds in the missing granddaughter's inheritance.

There was a letter, too, for Lester. It was marked "personal," and sealed. The lawyer handed it to him, said Helen had given it to him a few months back. Then the nurse reminded them that Lester was due to get some sleep, and everybody left his room.

It was true that Lester was exhausted. It tired him out just to open the letter, so he put the envelope on the bedside stand so he could take a look at its contents later. While he slept, the compulsively tidy night nurse put it into the little basket containing all the other personal belongings they'd send home with him in a few days.

· · ·

After his heart attack, it was like there were two Lester Brecks instead of one. One was familiar to Ellie and Stella, in fact to everyone who had ever known him. This was the hearty man who always enjoyed a good story and a good laugh. The man who knew a thousand and one stories about Heaven's history. The man who could hold forth pleasantly and equally with the denizens of Pete's Gate and First United. The man who accepted with equanimity that he'd been swindled right out of house and home by the woman he'd lived with for more than fifty years.

Now, with Helen gone, another Lester emerged to alternate with the first. It wasn't that Helen possessed him, but rather that her difficult presence had always required his most gracious and positive response. In the absence of her influence, it was as if some invisible set of restraints had been cut, and Lester was sent lurching so far in the direction of his life-loving tendencies that he went right past them to another realm, the morose and disappointed part of himself. Like a bungee jumper at the end of his rope, Lester bounced between this new self and his old one.

During the long stays by his bedside, Ellie had watched these moods take Lester, then fling him back again to the gentle humor and relaxed manner everyone called his "true self." When she saw him leave the familiar places and look into his unlit corners, it worried her. Lester welcomed her in his good moods, and withdrew from her in the bad times. Sometimes Nadja could cheer him up, but sometimes nobody could get through his gloom. Then, Ellie would check with Stella for a favorite recipe and see if she couldn't lead him back via food.

To tell the truth, Lester hadn't eaten well in the whole time he'd been married to Helen. Helen was organized, she was efficient, she was a whiz with numbers, she could manage the farm like nobody's business. But she could burn coffee, and overcook peas till the only thing left of them was a salty mash. Her cakes never rose properly, her casseroles always lacked some essential ingredient, the fibers of her pot roast stood strong, firm, and well apart from each other, like dental floss in the inevitably greasy and tasteless gravy. All those years living on Helen's cooking, with just a meal a week at Clara's Kitchen, had kept Lester pretty trim. And the years of hard farm labor and sleeping in the barn had added strength and stamina.

The fact is, Ellie was destroying Lester with kindness. He was gaining weight, which might have been good up to a point, but he went beyond that point. And he just sat in the big nubby green chair in the living room. Ellie had taken on the chore of feeding the chickens while Lester was in the hospital; the pigs had been sold right after Helen's will was read. The vegetable garden was mostly poke and pigweed now. All the fields were leased out to neighboring farmers. There was nothing left for Lester to do.

People really didn't know quite what to make of it. They'd always assumed that if Lester managed to outlive Helen, he'd enjoy life even more.

. . .

It was August. Ellie had marked her fortieth birthday a couple months earlier while Lester was still in the hospital. She was noticing that her feet hurt in the morning when she first got up. She was also noticing that her period was light for the second month in a row. God, she thought, I'm not hitting menopause already, am I?

Nadja noticed something, too. The glass plant had closed down for remodeling, and her weekend plate-reading business was booming, so she was treating herself to some days off before looking for new employment. She'd been coming in regularly for lunch at Clara's Kitchen. On one particular day, Ellie had joined her at a table for a spell, then had jumped up to ring up a customer waiting to leave. Nadja glanced at the nearly untouched sandwich on Ellie's plate, watched Ellie move sluggishly between the table and the cash register, back to the kitchen to pick up a soup and salad special, over to the table where Seese sat writing in her journal, then back to the kitchen to fetch the pot of freshly brewed coffee. When she made it back to refill their cups, Nadja looked at Ellie, perplexed and even a little incredulous. "When," said Nadja, "did you find the time to get pregnant? And with who?"

Ellie was immobilized by the thought. She stood stock-still until Nadja was almost afraid she was going to fall over. Then she turned her head and looked around the restaurant to make sure no one had heard Nadja's words. "Is that what this is?" Ellie asked quietly, and Nadja nodded.

"Sure looks like it."

"Shit," breathed Ellie. "Shit, shit, shit."

"Is it Lester?" Nadja matched Ellie's voice level. They both knew this was something to keep out of Seese's range.

"It might be," Ellie allowed, "but I doubt it." Nadja had that amazing ability to not raise her eyebrows at an answer like that. "It's probably the guy from Detroit whose Dad had surgery while Lester was in ICU. It's a broken condom in any case. I'm not stupid," Ellie said. "Just doomed."

"Oh, Ell," Nadja sighed. "Ellie, Ellie, Ellie."

Then Bobby called for a warm-up on his coffee, and Ellie, taking a deep breath, turned determinedly back to her job.

Later that night she stopped by Nadja and Granny's.

Nothing was clear.

"That's because you aren't clear," Granny explained. "If you decide what to do, even if you don't think you've decided, it'll show up. If you haven't decided, it won't."

"If you get an abortion," Nadja added, "you might want to go all the way up to South Bend or even Chicago. I would, if I were you. Will you tell Lester?"

159

"I don't know," Ellie frowned. "Maybe it would give the old man something to live for."

"Excuse me," Nadja said, "but that seems to me like a piss-poor reason to have a baby. I can tell you that much for sure."

Granny just looked worried.

Ellie regarded Nadja.

"How do you do it, really?" she asked.

"Do what?"

"Tell from people's leftovers what's going on." She'd asked once before, years ago, but she didn't recall getting a satisfactory answer. Maybe she'd be able to do it herself. Maybe then she could stare at her plate and know what to do next, instead of just stare at her plate, period.

"A combination of things. Some of it's intuition. Most of it's just paying attention. Not just to what's going on at the moment of the reading, but paying attention all the time, tucking things away, knowing where to find them when the time comes. But also watching a person's eyes, their body language, how they respond to what you say. People tell you a lot even when you don't ask them to."

Ellie nodded. She'd been thinking about that. She'd been thinking, too, of things she knew about Nadja without having been told. She'd had some intuitions of her own. They didn't seem to have much to do, however, with the problem at hand.

· · ·

At night, Ellie would lie in bed next to Lester and try to fit her body into the indentation in the mattress that Helen had left. She would listen to Lester's steady snore and marvel at her predicament. Sometimes the snoring kept her awake and she would feel a special kinship with the departed Mrs. Breck. "No wonder she made him sleep in the barn," Ellie would think, smiling in spite of the tightness in her jaw.

At other times a tenderness for Lester overcame her, and she would lie awake silently crying. She wanted to take care of him. She wanted to bring him back to life. The fix she was in stemmed, perhaps, from that attempt.

Lester and Ellie had been off-again, on-again lovers ever since their trip to the midway. The first few months, he'd come all the way through the passage, up through her house to the bedroom. Later, their increasing instinct for circumspection led them to move their liaisons back to the small chamber of the basement. Ellie furnished it with scented candles and a mattress, and a portable tape player for romantic music.

Usually, Lester would visit Maurice after supper and stay until it was closing time at Clara's Kitchen. After Ellie made sure Stella had driven home, she would dial Maurice's number and let it ring twice. That was Lester's signal to head down the alley to the garage, pull aside the floorboards, and climb down the little ladder into the tunnel. The next morning, he would retrace his steps, making his way back via the underground passage to the garage. Then, while Ellie walked down the street in full view of the busybodies who kept an eye on things, Lester detoured four blocks through back alleys to Maurice's garage, where he kept his car stored. He'd check in on Maurice, then drive back to Clara's for his coffee about ten minutes after the doors opened, when there might be one or two others there to see him arrive.

This sense of adventure had vanished when Lester came out of the hospital, and at first he hardly seemed interested in a physical relationship with Ellie. But she coaxed him with back rubs and funny stories about the ladies at Sue Ellen Sue's House of Beauty, and eventually he was willing to ask her into his bed. It was strange doing it there, where Helen had slept. Even Lester hadn't slept in that bed for much of his married life.

But the deep sadness that clung to Lester she could never fully dispel.

. . .

Lester stands in front of the mirror and practices dying. He actively attempts to drain the color from his face, but his efforts backfire, and instead he takes on a distinctly ruddy tone. He holds his heart — clutches it, really, but then is embarrassed at looking like Red Foxx doing his Sanford routine. He chuckles to himself at the idea that he might in any way look like Redd Foxx. He thinks about a record he heard once — good God, it must have been at least thirty-five years ago — at Maurice's house. Redd Foxx announcing a horse race — what were those horses' names? There was Kleenex by a nose, he recalled, and something about My Dick stretching into the lead that kept the young boys who gathered conspiratorially around the record player in the back room convulsed with suppressed laughter. Suppressed, because Maurice was the type who would burst into a room from which too much teenage energy seeped out, and raise hell. And that he did, confiscating his son's record and ordering him and his pals to go find something worthwhile to do instead of listening to trash like that, unless, of course, he wanted Maurice to call his mother and tell her what kind of nonsense he and his friends were up to. Then Maurice had put the record back on the turntable, just to see what the boys were listening to, and he and Lester laughed at the off-color puns till tears came to their eyes. Well, Lester thinks now, I got off track there. Sorry, folks, he mutters to his reflection, and considers again how best to die.

I could choke, he thinks, but is distracted yet again, this time considering the possibility of being embraced from behind by Miss December, skilled in the Heimlich maneuver. But he shakes her off, again regains his focus, and gives choking a try. He inhales deeply, expels the air, then clamps his hands around his neck. But a few seconds of stopped breath bring such a rapidly rising panic that he gasps and abandons his effort.

This is no good, thinks Lester. There isn't a one of these ways that doesn't make me feel like a first-rate fool. But God! I'm tired of living!

Lester takes a last baleful look at himself in the bathroom mirror. I look like Death already, he thinks. If I'm alive, I should at least look alive.

He turns from the mirror now and shuffles down the hallway to the bedroom. There on Helen's dresser are all of her things, exactly as she left them. Ellie had suggested cleaning them off, but Lester clung to them, as if they were part of a sacred shrine, so Ellie had to find other nooks in the room for her own artifacts.

He searches among the bottles, vials, jars and tubes, and finally finds what seems to him a shade of health. He rubs the rouge into his cheeks, and then, to blend the effect, rubs a bit more on the rest of his face. The new ruddiness offsets the grey of his eyebrows, but he colors them brown again with the mascara. The nose hairs have to go, but with those little scissors. No way will he tweeze them out the way she did hers. It can't be good for you to do that. The tip of the scissors tickles, and Lester involuntarily twitches away from the sensation. And with that abrupt move, the scissors puncture the thin skin inside his left nostril.

Cursing, Lester drops the scissors and slams a Kleenex against the small flow of blood and pain. He recovers his calm, then checks his smile. It's good-looking, one definite advantage of having false teeth. With his left hand, he continues to press lightly against the injured nostril. With his right, he decides to use the mascara brush, touch up his hair a bit, especially around the temples. One stroke leads to another, and soon the grey is minimal.

Finally, gingerly, he removes the tissue. The bleeding has stopped. He regards himself in his dead wife's bureau mirror: ruddy complexion, grey hair reduced to a just a few distinguished touches, one nostril still too hairy, but he decides not to risk another wound.

His neck, leathery from years in the sun, betrays him. He sights the anti-wrinkle cream jar, slathers the stuff on, and turns up his collar while it goes to work.

It's not a logical thought for a man determined to die, but it occurs to Lester that he should put some antibiotic cream on the cut. There's a little tube of it somewhere. Probably in that basket of things they sent back with him from the hospital. He walks back to the bathroom and finds the little plastic basket sitting on the second shelf of the towel closet. There's that little tube of cream — right next to a letter. What letter is that? I don't remember getting any letters in the hospital. He dabs a tiny bit of antibiotic up his nose, and examines the envelope. It's Helen's handwriting. "Personal," it says. I'll take a look at it later, see what it says.

By the time he's gotten downstairs, and has walked in careful, deliberate steps to his favorite nubby-green overstuffed chair, he's forgotten the letter again. He sits down, lets it drop to his lap, composes himself, and waits to die a handsome death.

"What in the world are you doing?" Ellie stops and shifts her sagging bag of groceries from right hip to left. There sits Lester, like an aging queen, or the bearded lady dressed to entertain admirers in her tent. Lester blinks slowly and smiles a bit stupidly. Like the Cheshire Cat, thinks Ellie. Maybe he'll disappear now.

She is suddenly overwhelmed with a desire for him to disappear. The contrast between the new life taking shape inside her and this sad, sagging man, insisting on death, is intolerable.

It is one of those moments. Mystics call it a shift in consciousness. Others simply refer to something snapping. Moorings cut loose, bearings giving way. The future, or at least one version of it, is not so much seen as felt, and the feeling — dread — is all it takes for you to know you'd choose *anything* else. Ellie sways from the impact of the realization and sees herself as one of those dying poplars in the windbreak along Lester's driveway. A *no* comes up from her belly and down from her brain. Roots or no, I will die in Heaven never having known Earth. It can't be. And she begins to grieve. With her grocery bag sliding off her hip and tears overflowing her eyes, Ellie mourns the end with Lester.

Lester doesn't understand. "I'm sorry," he says. "I'm a foolish old man."

Ellie shakes her head softly. "No," she tells him. "You do what you need to do." And she turns from him gently, so as not to alarm him, and asks over her shoulder as she walks to the kitchen, "What would you like for dinner?"

"Chicken-fried steak," says Lester, without the least hesitation.

Moments later, as she breads the cutlet, Lester's eyes close and his chin drops to his chest, rests there against the turned-up shirt collar. He snores. Ellie's tears salt the meat and spatter the hot cooking oil.

She brings him a TV tray so he doesn't have to get up. "Aren't you eating?" he asks. She says she's not really hungry tonight. She's never been hungrier, but it's not for food. No need for him to know that.

When the meal is over, Ellie excuses herself, saying she has some laundry to fold. She thinks fleetingly of packing a bag, but then an old song begins to play in her head. *You got to move*, it cautions her, *when the spirit say move*. Now she realizes she is a refugee, and must take only what she can wear. She goes to the bedroom, pulls on three extra pair of clean underwear and adds a blouse over her tank top. It is warm tonight, but later it will cool down. She ties the sleeves of her old cardigan around her waist, sits down on the bed, looks slowly around the room mouthing silent goodbyes to her miniature horses, the ledger, the lace, the newspaper clipping, her boxes of maps, her Emily Dickinson poems. She says goodbye to the indentation in the bed where Lester sleeps. Dear Lester.

Are you ready? She addresses the question silently to the quickening life in her belly. "Me too," she says aloud, and stands.

Downstairs, Lester is dozing again. Ellie writes him a note: "Forgot coffee, be right back," it says. When she takes the note in to tuck into his lap, where he'll be sure to find it, Helen's letter is there, still patiently waiting its turn. "Personal," it says. Whatever it is, Ellie thinks, it's Lester's story, not mine. The sudden thought takes her by surprise. She tucks her note into the open edge of the envelope.

Back in the kitchen, she is about to wash up the few dishes when she notices the patterns on Lester's plate. The bit of steak, she supposes, is Lester. The trace of gravy must be her. The trace runs across the surface of the dish, following a flat path toward the edge. And who, then, would the third scrap be? That piece of string bean that sits near the meat?

Ellie leaves a note for Nadja under Lester's dirty plate. "Take care of him," it says. "I'll write you from Somewhere Else." Then she takes the new can of coffee from the shelf, slips it into her purse, and steps out the back door.

It is dusk. Fireflies are just beginning to show, one here, one there. Their modest lights seem to mark a path to the distant unknown. One flashes by the car door. Ellie opens the door, climbs in and pulls the door almost closed; she saves the slamming for further down the driveway. She releases the emergency brake and floors the clutch pedal. The car rolls slowly forward. Halfway to the road, it stops. That's it for hills in Heaven, thinks Ellie. She looks back at the farmhouse. Lester is in there dozing. He'll call Nadja. Nadja will see the undone dishes. She'll find the note. She probably knows already that I'm leaving. Another sudden thought: a memory of swings and candy-bar wrappers. She's known all along. She's known since we were nine. Chicago. She said Chicago.

Dear Nadja. We are finally trading lives, you and I. I bequeath you Heaven. I accept your freedom. Dear Lester. Goodbye.

166

She starts the car and does not wait to see if the noise wakes him up. She turns right at the end of the driveway, and follows the dusty road to the corner where the sign points left to the center of Heaven and right to Maple Grove. Ellie stops, looks each way, then shifts into first, then second, third, and fourth, and drives forward, following the fireflies. Dust rises behind her, obscuring all vision of the past. The fireflies are thick with promise now, and their lights are everywhere.

JAN MAHER, a native of central Indiana, now makes her home in the Pacific Northwest. She holds a Ph.D. in Interdisciplinary Studies: Theater, Education, and Neuroscience, and teaches education at Heritage College and Western Washington University. Her plays include *Widow's Walk,* which gained finalist status in the Actors Theatre of Louisville Ten-Minute Play Contest, and *Intruders and Ismene,* published by Rain City Projects. She writes curriculum materials, often in collaboration with her husband and fellow writer/educator Douglas Selwyn. Her poetry, short fiction, and essays have appeared in several small literary and educational journals. *Heaven, Indiana* is her first novel.